CROSSING OVER
and other tales

CROSSING OVER
and other tales

#$%_&'()*!+"#$%_&'()*!+"#$%_
$%_&'()*!+"#$%_&'()*!+"#$%_&
%_&'()*!+"#$%_&'()*!+"#$%_&'
_&'()*!+"#$%_&'()*!+"#$%_&'(
&'()*!+"#$%_&'()*!+"#$%_&'()

RICHARD ELMAN

!+"#$%_&'()*!+"#$%_&'()*!+"#
+"#$%_&'()*!+"#$%_&'()*!+"#$
"#$%_&'()*!+"#$%_&'()*!+"#$%
#$%_&'()*!+"#$%_&'()*!+"#$%_
$%_&'()*!+"#$%_&'()*!+"#$%_&
%_&'()*!+"#$%_&'()*!+"#$%_&'
_&'()*!+"#$%_&'()*!+"#$%_&'(
&'()*!+"#$%_&'()*!+"#$%_&'()
'()*!+"#$%_&'()*!+"#$%_&'()*
()*!+"#$%_&'()*!+"#$%_&'()*!
)*!+"#$%_&'()*!+"#$%_&'()*!+

Charles Scribner's Sons
New York

FOR SUSEY CRILE

Printed in the United States of America
Library of Congress Catalog Card Number 72-1191
SBN 684-13021-1 (cloth)

Books by Richard Elman

Crossing Over and Other Tales

Fredi & Shirl & the Kids

An Education in Blood

The Reckoning

Lilo's Diary

Charles Booth's London
(with Albert Fried)

Ill-at-Ease in Compton

The 28th Day of Elul

The Poorhouse State:
The American Way of Public Assistance

A Coat for the Tsar

Contents

CROSSING OVER
and other tales

PART 1

CROSSING OVER

An ordinary life can be a disaster. You don't despise people any less for not being very much at all. They are people, and we all make errors, some of us, of course, more than others. If only they knew there were others making errors just like themselves they would be no less ordinary. But they are not our peers, or friends, just our brothers.

When my own particular long lost brother Joseph Perkell was born he was not considered ordinary by the ordinary people who populated our household. They considered him extraordinary. Could anybody say they were wrong? He was certainly bigger than they were in some respects, and they were certainly not midgets at all. As older brother, I was a bit of a gnome, though certainly not a midget either.

At the time I was seven, five years my brother's senior, and we had very little in common to begin with. It was not surprising this should be so but it was upsetting to him, for I thought I should love him, and he always said he loved me. Those, in fact, were his very first words at birth.

"I love you, Joseph." The red-faced boy, my brother.

I did not immediately return the feeling. I was not in love with anybody, certainly not a red-faced boy of two who went around claiming to be my brother.

The family was naturally quite upset. He was said to be bigger than me already and growing like a weed. What did I have to show to them for all their pains? I must try to love my brother.

Loving Joseph was never very easy. He was the sort of

infant who was always getting in the way of things. Like myself, for example. Joseph always made me feel as if I owed him something. For what? Being so much smaller than he was nothing to feel that badly about. I was just so much older that it couldn't be helped.

Nor could it be helped that we sometimes felt together as if there was something approaching liking between us. It is many years since it last happened and what it felt like I do not remember, though it was nice.

None of our many parents, of course, approved. They wanted us to be nice to each other, but not to like each other. At least not openly. It got everybody in the house so nervous when we were that upset.

The really difficult period came between us when it was time to assign roles, and careers. As older brother I was certain to be an engineer. My function would be to design those bridges that my late brother Joseph was so determined to cross over. He wished simply to get to the other side, wherever that was, but as I was pretty anxious to get there too, this made for difficult complications in design and stress.

Of course, my brother Joseph said he would go first. Of course, I agreed, since he was the youngest, but first, would you let me, I added, design it.

Not at all, he said, crossing over into nowhere, quickly, by himself. Needless to say he was very very lonely there but he did not fall all the way down and when he did there was always somebody around to catch him. Joseph called what we had just done together our span together. He then asked me if I would help design another for him to be all alone.

Our parents were, to be very sure, upset with the idea that one so old as myself could dare to contrive for one so young, all alone, and they, of course, suggested that we try next time to work in concert, too, as sibling to sibling. The problem might also be solved with pontoons.

Joseph said I had come up with none worth standing on and I said Joseph you are a damn fool. The question isn't floating here or there but flying over the water to the moon and stars.

Never in my life, said my ornery little brother who was doomed to live forever.

We went back to work at being brothers again.

By now I was nearly forty-eight and Joseph who had once been my younger brother was at least fifty-six. Together we had meant so much to each other, but we were not now, for different reasons.

I can remember the time Joseph said it could be very different with us if we would only design another bridge, with a definite blueprint in advance, and lots of supplies of iron beams, rivets, nuts, spanners, bolts, stanchions, and what-have-yous to get across.

I wasn't what you might call in disagreement. However, I also thought I was pretty brilliant, and also pretty busy.

Joseph couldn't seem to understand any of this at all.

We parted then and went our separate ways, myself going off to Italy to study the works of the great masters, while Joseph remained at home turning somersaults into the air until such time as I could return and we could relate face to face, as one brother to another.

That it never happened is as much a function of my careless indolence as of Joseph's spectacular turnabouts on the various rigmaroles of his profession. We were such brothers it could not possibly be any other way.

It was as if the moon wanted to come down out of the clouds but did not know how. It could be said equally, I suppose, that the clouds had blotted out the moon for a spell, though that did not seem to matter.

My first thought was to give up entirely. I thought of that again and again in the intervals between trying to bring Joseph around to my way of thinking. Meanwhile, as I say, our parents fumed.

Then it occurred to me to stop lying altogether, but how would that help Joseph, and our parents, and all our other friends? Surely they needed to lie with me as much as myself, and with whom and about whom did not seem to matter so long as the lie was good enough, which I had insisted all along it was. They sometimes said, for example, it's our misfortune and none of your own, but I always insisted it was a common misfortune, particularly so with Joseph.

It seemed as if a dramatic gesture was called for that would not scare people half to death. On the brightest day of all I would announce to the world that my brother Joseph was *the* most accomplished crosser over I had ever known to exist. In fact I could become his press agent. In the world of our parents that was still considered important. The question was would Joseph.

Another important question was about myself. Did I have the right to exist side by side with such a brother when I was always being asked to kiss his ass in public which, of course, I should have done gladly, if no other role for me had been available.

We had come to a parting of our ways. Joseph and his various friends were going off somewhere. In time I would join them with our parents, if only I knew how. Meantime, there were all the other little gnomes and midgets to think about, including myself.

I decided to take an advertisement on the front page of the *New York Times*: MY BROTHER JOSEPH IS THE WORLD'S GREATEST BRIDGE CROSSER I HAVE EVER KNOWN AND ALL I EVER DID WAS SIT AND WATCH.

As if everybody hadn't known that all along.

When this didn't work I decided to hold a press conference to announce that I was scared to death of Joseph and his stunts and wouldn't somebody please help us to get along with each other.

A child offered herself in public but I was much too afraid of getting her into trouble with her mother for being out so late.

A black crow flew in through my open window, then, one bright sunny day and said, HELP ME, I'M A BLACKBIRD, AND I'LL HAVE ONE FOR THE ROAD WITH YOU.

That seemed like taking such advantage of the misfortunes of others that I said: GET OUT OF MY LIFE UNLESS I CAN FLY YOU ACROSS ON MY WINGS, OR YOUR WINGS, OR BOTH.

The crowd of midgets and gnomes congregating every day outside my window was truly getting fierce.

Their leader was a certain Julia Pierce.

I pleaded with her not to make me do a thing like that, but when I did it again she said it's too late already, now you'll have to do it like this.

Or else, she said, just come down out of that house and I'll show you a thing or two.

I could show you a thing or two myself, I said, but she said frankly, I doubt that, and there we were again, and again, and again, like brothers, and sisters, now and forever.

I guess that's how I got to be such a student of human nature, though if you ask me I prefer building bridges any day of the week, especially next Tuesday, when I'm scheduled to be five years old again.

As for my brother Joseph he's been gone a long long time ago when he was my friend and there's not much I can do about that except cry out occasionally, I LOVE YOU, JOSEPH, WHEREVER YOU ARE.

And maybe hope for a postcard back now and then.

OLD OLD FRIENDS

Once upon a time when he was a man and she was a woman they got lost somehow and couldn't find each other anymore, and he kept trying to find her again with everybody he met, and she was trying to do the same thing, and they found words, or feelings, for which there were no words, nothing to hang words on; and he went out and tried to find himself with other people and he kept finding her, and she could not be that way for him anymore, and he was crazy.

They said, "We must learn to be by ourselves." But they found they were quite alone.

They crowded others into their lives and they crammed them in and they felt stiff and cramped and they were completely unhappy.

She had to be by herself for the first time in her life, and he would have to wait. He waited such a long time but she never came back.

He never should have waited that long.

He went out among his friends, but either they were all gone, or they were afraid of him. They didn't know him anymore because he wouldn't show himself to them. He was still waiting.

They went out into the world without him, into time, and he went along with the feeling that his time was running out.

They said, "You must be patient."

But first he had to wait for this one, and then for that one; he couldn't anymore.

He was alone.

He wanted to be with his friends in time.

He thought she had to be in time with him.

They could not be together.

He grew angry, and bitter. He gave off little presents of rage to all his friends.

He was that lonely when he went away from all his friends that he could never see any of them anymore without feeling they were his old friends.

He went out to them again and they were just friends. They took him back in where he was still lonely.

Now they were all friends with each other and he was only friendly with a memory of himself and her.

He went out among his friends prepared to die.

The memory of friendship was not strong enough to supplant her memory.

He was by now totally insane.

He was prepared to die.

He was alone, just as he had been at birth.

He wanted either to be reborn, or to die.

He was also prepared to have a friend.

He knew how he had lived for thirty-seven years with another prisoner by his side and that when they were released he was alone because he had to remain behind to keep the door closed, or open.

He went away from himself for a little while, with this

one or that one, but he would always have to come back because he was that alone.

He needed himself so badly. He tried to liberate the other person he needed and she was just another prisoner.

Alone, he went away from himself again.

THE BALLAD OF THE LONG-LEGGED ICHTHYOLOGIST

The lady poet left only her poems, and no earrings. That was reserved for the long-legged ichthyologist. And the doctor of ophthalmic medicine left behind an eye heavily bedewed with teardrops. They were all saying, "Call me sometime." Who? When? How? Where?

As if he really could respond just to an eye, some bead dangles, a few poems, without having to face the ladies one by one also.

Then what?

He knew all about himself. Always looking for the mother he'd never had.

What about them?

A man is more than just the sum of all his parts, he kept telling himself, and so is any woman. If so, then what?

There were the beads on the night table. The eye in the medicine glass. The poems downstairs in the mailbox with his keys still dangling.

Call me again
Call me sometime please
Call me

It was all that simple. Well, perhaps for a simple man it was, though not for him. He was, as usual, confused by the possibility of happiness much more than by all the old-fashioned certainties of unhappiness.

He got up and read the eye, and wrote a poem, and fondled the beads and was immediately uneasy, sick to his stomach. The feeling that he was just much too dependent on this sort of thing. To be so dependent all of a sudden on what he had always known all along was beyond his reach. Such as friendship . . .

He stuffed the beads into an envelope and her poems into another pocket, put the eye in a locket which he kept for such purposes that he always wore dangling around his neck, and went off to see his psychiatrist.

"You're crazy, Richard. Give me those things before you hurt yourself," said the four times married Ph.D. with the beard. "I'm putting you back on monogamy for a while. You're getting dangerous. You're a hazard to the entire community. Now just you cut it out, *hear?*"

"Fuck you," he told Dr. Kagan, and went around town delivering his little packets of souvenirs to the doormen of all and sundry.

Tomorrow he was planning to make dates to see a veterinarian, a doctor of pharmacy, a hooker, a cook, a chorus girl, and a free-lance professional mother.

As he finished dialing all the various numbers and put down the phone he reflected to himself he had surely reached the point where it was becoming possible, any day now, to begin to make some choices.

ON MAKING FRIENDS

A friend is usually somebody you get to know because you just can't seem to know anybody else.

I don't mean never. Knowing somebody like a friend is always possible once or twice in your life. In my case I never had pets so I was forced to have friends. But now that I have either mislaid or given away all my oldest pets I have nothing but friends left to choose from, and I'm not even too sure I have that many of them.

Not too sure means not unsure of myself with others, though, for that matter, not that sure of myself. The friend indeed who is the friend in need is not what I am really talking about, but of the luxury of having more than one, suddenly, breaking out everywhere all around you, like hives or pets. Of the lot I think I like some of the girls quite a bit, though not too many of those others. That's because I'm so flirtatious I don't know what to do with myself a lot of the time except to pet my friends, like this, or that, as if my pets were friends, and my friends pets, or, maybe, the other way around.

I think I am really just trying to say that a man, any man, is more than just the sum of all his parts, and so it is true equally for most, if not all, women, unless I'm mistaken, but I am never more than I was on the day I first mislaid Likitha.

Little Likitha, I should say, or perhaps Licky. She was my pet longer than any of the others and she somehow got pretty badly mislaid, I'll never know where, except that we had something in common once or twice. What was it? Nothing more or less than an exchange of mutual tenderness. I honestly loved having Licky cuddling next to me, and when she was unhappy so was I. Those were some of our happiest moments. But, eventually, she, too, got mislaid, just like all the others, and there began the miseries for both of us.

"Since you've mislaid me, don't complain if you can't find us anymore," she told me. "I just might be elsewhere."

I thought she was probably a lot more than maybe correct about that, though where she was exactly I could not be sure. There was also the problem of where I was, and who had, after all, mislaid me.

On the twenty-first day of the month of the Fish I made an understanding with myself: that I would no more allow myself to choose to be Licky's keeper and guardian than she would me.

It subsequently rained for nearly a whole week until even a pet like her had to go outside, if for no other reason than to take a breath of water.

She did not return until the following Cancer.

By then I had been pretty badly mislaid so many times that I was just plain awfully glad to see her.

Of course, we quarreled, but later I fed her from a china bowl with little blue flowers and cuddled until dawn.

That is to say she cuddled in my arms, though I, being so much bigger, found it just extremely difficult cuddling with her.

And besides it was so often resented.

Don't I really mean to suggest by this brief memoir that pets are my best substitute for friends? They are just sometimes the only substitute.

And now that I find I have plenty of both I have neither.

It's a dog's life, I guess, and if not, why not?

Or, as I whispered into Licky's ear when she returned: "Now that you are back where will you get mislaid next?"

MYSELF AND THE TUGOMAN

My dearest friend in the world was once so much bigger than me that often when we walked together on the street she had to bend all the way over just to hear me say "I love you."

Not that I am so small. But that's the way it is between men and women. I was her father. She was not my little girl. She was another man's mistress and my friend. I loved her, though I didn't often understand her. She called me her friend so much it hurt. We label this initial perspicacity romance; afterward it is sometimes followed by other feelings.

Forever after our initial intimacies we remained strangers. It was as if a child had put her hand to fire. We shrank from our passion for each other. I don't know why, don't know what I feared she feared. Her tenderness I feared as much as I feared anything, and I assure you I feared everything.

On the last day of the month of Tish a great festival was going to be held in the principal city of our small galaxy and I invited Florence to be my guest. She said she could not. It was one thing to mourn something that had passed between us; quite another thing to celebrate.

I went alone, like a child without his mother, fearful, timorous, intrepid, and during the feasting that preceded the orgy drank more than I should have, ending up exceedingly blotto. My eyes were all bloodshot and a former business friend suggested a patch.

So it was, with my left eye closed behind a square of black silk, and my body entirely unclothed, I encountered Florence, naked, among the revelers.

"But what are you doing here?"

She smirked. "Did you think it was past my bedtime?"

"You said you didn't wish to celebrate with me."

She placed her hands under her full breasts so that they thrust out toward me and wagged her hips in the manner of the Sardoettes, a people in our galaxy who are rarely visited these days. "That did not preclude another," Florence said. "Did you think I was going to sit home like a stick in the mud?"

Suddenly I found myself as angry as I had ever been. I grabbed Florence and held her close in my arms. "I'm tired of the soak of sex," I said, "and equally of the zonk. I'm tired, too, of your fickleness . . ."

"To refuse an invitation is not being fickle," the dear girl explained. "It is simply my way of discriminating . . ."

I demanded to meet her escort.

"Of course."

Florence produced a rather attractive four-foot-one-inch Tugoman with skin so ebony it was almost purple and a triple row of double chins beneath his chin and also teeth, and also across his belly, above his private parts.

"Florence has told me so much about you," he said, bowing toward me with a smile, as if I was even smaller, "I feel as if I already know you," and, of course, he took her hand and they waddled away together then.

Needless to say I did not see them again for the rest of that evening.

Left to myself, I tried to make friends with a woman of the Clitos. They are a race of short-haired females with pouting lips who are said to be very sensitive to touch, even though their skins may be rather coarse.

She told me her name was Semele. In a way I thought she was rather beautiful, sufficiently so that we could make love, and afterward she held me very close and called me her "frog," her "toad," her "prince of sudden leaps." But then she asked that I kiss her in a place where I do not usually kiss strangers from a foreign nation, and we parted barely friends.

It was rather late in the evening. The vessel would be arriving very shortly to return us to our galaxy and I knew if I wanted company with me through space I had better act impetuously and swiftly, for once in my life.

With all the energy I could summon I approached a beautiful young creature from Nubula. It was not hard to tell she was impressed with my figure, though I did not know if we might also orgiate.

"You were with the lovely young friend of the Tugoman," she observed. "I saw how you two argued so fiercely. You must love each other very much to be so hostile . . ."

"It's not so simple as all that," I explained, as if echoing the words of my former shrinkopath. "We were once friends. She might have been my daughter, the child of my young love, and now I see her with a perfect stranger . . ."

"Yes, he is rather perfect," she sighed, and smiled demurely, "for a Tugoman of course . . . What's the matter? Don't you find him attractive?"

"Of course!"

I could tell she thought I was aroused because she wet her lips in a specifically sensual manner with just the tip of her tongue.

It is never quite so simple in my case. I need to know a person for a few minutes, quite a few, say five, or ten, before I can allow myself such liberties, and besides, I had never been with a creature from Nubula, and was unsure of their anatomical construction.

I am not a man who enjoys fumbling. To be self-assured in such situations is, I assure you, simply a matter of further and further intimacies, both above and below the line of sight.

I wet my lips and smiled back at the lovely Nubulan who had, for the moment, disappeared, only to return again.

". . . And now you wish to intimate with me, I suppose," she said, "and perhaps we can also conjugal?"

"It is only so I will not travel through space alone," I assured her. "I thought you would like to take the trip with me."

"If only I could," she sighed. "But I have the clap, a Venutian . . . and you seem to have something wrong with your eye. Is it infected?"

"Not as much as it will be," I said, and left her angrily.

The trip back to earth was as difficult as lifting the proverbial moat, and equally dissatisfying. I slept in the arms of

the stewardess, who was on call through most of the long in-
terstellar night and when it was time to depressurize over
the Azores my whole life flashed before me just as we were
coming down.

Florence was at the ramp to meet me.

She had, apparently, only been dawdling with her
Tugoman, for she had aged a bit. In fact, she assured me it
was simply a matter of the crow's feet, and asked could we
take breakfast together at that little place in Bangkok she
liked so much.

It was her birthday. Also the Day of Sighs, when one is
supposed to do nothing except enjoy the most licit fleshy
pleasures. In fact, there are really few such days on earth
when one is not, though Florence was almost childlike the
way she pleaded with me.

"Come. You know how much it pleases you," she said.
"Don't be such a stick in the mud . . ."

She handed me a lottery ticket she had purchased at the
barrier as a gift to welcome me home. "You will be rich if
you win."

"And if I lose . . ."

"We will be just as we once were," she said. "What
more can you ask?"

"I want to know you throughout the long night
ahead," I told her, "now, or forever, in Bangkok, too, if you
like . . ."

"That's quite impossible. After lunch," she told me, "I
have an appointment with a Chinaman. They are so clever

with vaginopuncture and I have been taking a great deal of vitamin E . . ."

"And what about me?" I demanded. "What about yours truly, alone, in Bangkok?"

"Your time will come," she said. "In fact someday we intend to liberate you, too. But first there are all the children we must be thinking about."

Florence put her arm through mine, and held me close, walking slowly off the ramp by my side. "You know I love you . . . and someday I want to have your child . . ."

"Of course. Either mine, or the Tugoman's . . ."

"Don't mention it," she said. "He snores. He recedes. He's a very obsessive person . . ."

"I love you *too*, Florence," I said then, "so very, very much . . ."

She said, "I think you mean *also*."

When the end of that day came we were in each other's arms above the polar ice. It was good to be so warm and secure together again. We landed at MacMurdoo. It is a long way from Thailand, I suppose, but really not so far as Tugomania.

EYES

Once I loved a woman with only one eye. Whenever we were together the other kept looking astray in the dark.

Her name to me was never very important. It was the tender ways we took each other in. She loved me as if there were no limits to our time together; I thought I knew better.

She died for me, at last. Beside my former wife I had her buried. It was a matter of some sentiment for me never to allow myself to remain so single-minded about just one person.

Then another woman came into my life, and demanded that I be with her for awhile. Once again our love knew of no limits except for the time we spent together; when this one died on me too, I decided to bury her apart because the small family plot was becoming overcrowded.

For awhile I remained all alone, taking my pleasures like a jackal. Always the smell of death was in my mouth. The one good eye I had could focus for a little while to assure me a kind of livid immortality with which I was always quite unhappy, but that other, which was so blue and clear and sharp, always saw more than it knew, or cared to know. It roamed the full range of my visions and fantasies, and often filled up with tears.

If only I had been a truly one-eyed man I might have suffered this grief almost gladly, and come to know the joyous exultation to be found after suffering, when one can draw another breath without pain, or even with pain, but also with joy and ease, and perhaps some pleasure. That was

23

never possible for one who lacked for nothing except coordination.

In those days the moon always wore a sallow cross-eyed look, and my friends were refusing to see me. I was very much alone with myself, peering out at strangers separately, between my two eyes. I saw and did much, though I learned little. The road I trod seemed paved with intentions. I had to shade each eye separately from the sun.

When I was forty I looked less than thirty. When I was fifty I could have been easily sixty. For awhile, then, the thing called life came into focus for me. For better or worse, I'd had a one; together or apart, I could still think of myself as a person.

I decided to test myself with Velma, who was so very very beautiful, only nineteen, but about as beautiful as most women can be at that age, and, too, she seemed to have a sort of crush on me: whereas other women had found the thing I did with my eyes disgusting, distressing, or both, Velma thought it was surely interesting. She assured me she could do the same with other people, but would prefer not to if only we would try to do it by ourselves together.

We were with each other seven whole months. During that time our eyes fused, and we went over the falls of love again and again, as if we were in a barrel together.

We were also sometimes tender with our bodies, and concerned.

The end of the world was scheduled for the sixth of June 1971. I remember that date because it was the day Velma said, "You are so good to me."

She reached out and plucked a piece of lint off my lapel. I was very frightened that Velma would go on to say something else. When she saw how pale my face was becoming her eyes began to water, and wander.

The sense of panic was mutual.

I wanted to touch Velma, somehow to assure her of my caring for her. In seizing her shoulders and pulling her close I broke the slim gold chain of a locket she always wore between her bosoms, and it fell to the floor.

"Now do you see what you've done," she snapped.

We were down on all fours together, looking for the locket, but it was no use. Her heart could be found, though the chain was in pieces, its tiny slim connecting links either twisted, or all smashed out flat.

When I came upright again, after brushing my knees clean of dirt, my eyes were everywhere in the room except with Velma; later, alone, I fell asleep.

Picture it as it really happened to me, to us. The end of the world never came. They put it off until the following March and by then Velma and I were no longer together. This didn't seem to matter very much.

Presently I am sixty-one, and looking for a nine-year-old girl with astigmatic vision.

Intentions—marriage.

(For B.M.)
I O U

Often I think when I'm not thinking at all I'm thinking much too much for my own damn good.

It's a matter of habit, not of knowing right from wrong. I've always known I was wronged, from birth, for no good reason. By habit. That's why I married Janine. She was better than me. She was smarter than me. She was also much much nicer than me. For no good reason that I know of she had agreed to live with me as man and wife.

That always made me feel pretty bad. To have one person like her usurp both roles in the marriage hurt more than I could ever say. I kept to myself and sulked.

The situation did not improve rapidly and after a month and a few days we were separated and divorced. Our haste was not precipitous, but a matter of some panic. We had come close to hating each other. Under the circumstances, we were hardly good companions, much less friends.

I was still what you might call a thinking man. The only trouble was I had nothing much left to think about, except Janine. It had never been my way, you see, to wallow in mere luxuries.

The next thing that happened we were remarried. All in all it was handled rather decorously this time. Since feeling almost anything could make me feel pretty badly, our prenuptial agreement stipulated nothing in respect to that.

We were now, for a brief while, perfect soul-mates. That is to say, we could correspond with each other from afar, or close up, and could live together, or apart, as equals. Peers. Our friends said they envied us. Our intimacies were never tenacious, or possessive, or despairing. Once, in a moment of passion, Janine cried out LUV . . .

I think she was in London at the time.

The only problem with our new relationship was I sometimes thought we should try to spend some time together.

Janine said, YOU JUST WANT TO BE CLOSE TO ANOTHER PERSON.

I couldn't disagree with her about that, either, because she happened to be in Moscow at the time.

While she was gone I sometimes brooded and occasionally saw other people. Then we were divorced for the second time. It was all my fault. I simply wished to make the separation seem a little less official. Again Janine pointed out, WHY NOT DIVORCE? IT'S SO MUCH LESS OLD-FOGEYISH AND IF WE CHANGE OUR MINDS, WE CAN ALWAYS BE REMARRIED AGAIN.

Of the two of us Janine was always more sensible.

In the brief interval between my second and third marriages to her I lived first with Helen Arp, a painter, and then with Milton Arp, her former husband, who was a writer. Really it was good to have other people in my life. I felt, at last, that I was making friends with the human race. That Helen and Milton were not on speaking terms simply meant I was required to relate to them as individuals, while they continued to relate to me as Archy.

Well, what else could I expect? They were Janine's friends. I was simply borrowing them while she was away.

For our third honeymoon we went to Rio. Janine had never been there with me.

From a spell in Sardinia she had come back exhausted. She still needed me, *now,* she said, more than ever.

WHY? I demanded. WHY ME?

ANYBODY ELSE WOULD DO, she explained, WHO WAS SO UNDEMANDING, BUT I DON'T HAPPEN TO KNOW ANYBODY ELSE LIKE THAT EXCEPT YOU.

I was really flattered.

By the next morning we were off again, on the night flight for Rio.

I sometimes think to have a real woman in my life is all I have ever desired from Janine, but then I know that can't be so. We have been married seven times, and seven times divorced, and if the in-between times were like holding my breath under water, the times we were together seemed no less stifling.

It was as if I had consented to just lie back and allow her to blow that hot spicy breath against my face without ever once demanding that she stop a moment so I could brush my teeth.

We had a relationship, I suppose, of sorts, but no romance, even though we sometimes tried.

Seven times the first hot rosy flush of feelings has taken us, and seven times we have responded, with caution, and tact, and candor, by being thoughtful.

The brutal truth is we never liked each other very much at all.

If only we had it might have all been over with a week-end.

CHAMBER MUSIC

I

She wanted to get rid of a husband, and I a wife. We got together. It wasn't lust. It wasn't love. More like mutual aid.

II

It turned out we really weren't that much better for each other than our previous mates had been, though in joining ourselves to this new yoke of woe we had somehow managed to shrug that other off.

"You are a man, and I believe I am a woman," she would say. "I don't understand."

"It's all too simple," I explained to Gilda. "We've accomplished just what we set out to do. Now let's say goodbye."

"Not on your life," she said, fiercely. "I love you, I love you."

She was lying on her side next to me in bed, singeing a few of the hairs on my chest with the glowing ember of her cigarette.

"Of course," she said, "I admit at first we were just using each other, but after awhile I began to feel something . . ."

"Yes . . . ?"

"Something I'd never felt before . . ."

"Ouch, that burns," I said. "Stop it!"

I turned my back to her.

I knew Gilda wasn't really lying. Was she, though, telling me the truth?

III

We were exactly the same age, I think. She worried a lot, about time, the time we were together, the time we weren't, and made of what time we had a continual quarrel over the time we were never to share.

For myself, time could not pass soon enough until I found myself with somebody I could truly serve forever, again, like the last time, which I have to admit was a total failure.

We were now, as I say, totally incompatible except for those rare moments when time would suddenly and inexplicably stop for us.

Gilda might ask then, lifting up her slim neck from the nest of reddish hair surrounding her bare white fragile shoulders, "What did you do that time? What happened?"

"Nothing very different . . ."

"It was so beautiful . . ."

"You mean that time."

I knew she did not mean the other times as well. Gilda was always blaming me with the good times we had together by comparing them favorably with the rest of those times that were so ordinary.

IV

When I fell in love with the dwarf she became exceedingly jealous.

"You spend all your time with *her,*" Gilda, blinking hard, said. "Can't you see? She's just not worthy of you."

"Gilda," I explained, "she is a he, and I don't spend all my time with Carol and you know it."

Faintly she smiled at me, as if trying out a new form of apology. "I never can tell with dwarfs . . ."

"It's the same as with males and females who are full-grown people. There are males and females. I don't see how you can say you can't tell. Carol is a male . . ."

"O you!"

Gilda went away, but she continued to believe my dwarf pal was female; and once when I protested too loudly that she must get the matter of Carol's sex straight or else just shut up about him, she called me sissy . . .

"That's what you are," she said. "A big sissy and a homo too . . ."

Then she began to cry, as if I had misled her to think otherwise.

The next time I saw her again was at a party where she had taken up with a giant. He was, at least, seven feet tall, with such large hands and feet he shambled like an ape.

"Benny," she said pertly, "this is my old friend Richy the writer. I told you about him the other evening . . ."

Either Benny was stupid, or else she had told him some pretty scurrilous things about me. The next thing I knew Benny socked me in the jaw. I went down and out and did not wake up again until the cab ride home with friends.

Early the next morning Gilda called.

"I'm sorry, darling. Does it hurt? I hope you got a taste of your own medicine. Now you know how I felt about Carol . . ."

"That's absurd," I said. "Carol is a he . . . and your damn friend near broke my jaw . . ."

"Think nothing of it," Gilda said. "Next time don't fall in love with dwarfs, and you can get even."

I don't think she ever got the message. There was only time left for us to go off elsewhere by ourselves.

On the day I did she sent me a one-word telegram: SCAREDY-CAT.

I went away.
She stayed behind.

I stayed behind.
She went away.

I went behind.
She stayed away.

V

It was getting both of us so crazy I even told Carol how I loved her.

First he was pretty angry because I thought he was a girl. He said just because he was a dwarf that was always happening to him.

"Think nothing of it," I told him. Then he was jealous that it should be Gilda again.

Next thing I knew he went up to Benny on the street and kicked him right in the shins.

I heard about it at brunch that Sunday. We were all wrestling with each other until one of us, I think it must have been Gilda, looked up through a bubble of blood on her face, and said, WHY IS EVERYBODY BEING SO CRAZY?

If anybody has a good answer to that question please tell me.

WHO KILLED
PRETTY BRILLIANT?

When the alarm clock awakens you in the morning you have three possibilities: to commit suicide, to go back to sleep, or to get up for work, or something else.

She was dead when I saw her the first time. Heart attack. I sort of liked the way she looked. It was the first time her face had come unfrozen. She'd made her choice.

It was not a brave act. Suicide by taking an overdose of sleeping pills is cowardly in comparison to sticking your head in a bucket of water. But she was just as dead. Dog food is good to a starving man, when the alternative is horse manure.

My name is Martin Kinnelly, 2221 Beechwood Drive, Daly City, California; I'm a private detective, which means my will is not completely free, just as the prices on a menu in a restaurant may cause you to prefer eating something you like less . . .   Pretty Brilliant was a client of my old friend, Ralph Royster, the well-known tree surgeon. Nothing can compel a man to do what he makes up his mind not to do. I took the case.

"But," you might inquire, "why was an excuse necessary?" You must realize there was a certain risk involved and I couldn't really help myself, either. My will was not entirely my own.

At this moment in time you are trying to decide whether to steal, embezzle, or hurt somebody in some way. Don't. There is no way any excuse is acceptable. You could be spanked, scolded, reprimanded, ostracized, criticized, discharged, severely punished, be shot, beaten up, electrocuted, hanged, quartered, or any number of things. You don't want this to happen if you can avoid it . . . which is where I come in, usually, as private dick.

When I came on the scene Pretty Brilliant was already rather dead. Her body could not be seen at all. Inside the chimney of the fireplace was her head. Two small fat legs stuck out across the bearskin rug into the living-room area along with the bottom hem of a rather flouncy skirt. Just as your background has no relation to the knowledge that three is to six what four is to eight, I didn't let the details bother me.

Well, you tell me, is God a reality, and is he good? About forty-seven per cent of the people I know have been stricken that way lately. Pretty Brilliant, in some respects, least of all.

She was dead. I came into her apartment, looked around, and guessed immediately it was murder. A pain in the ass. Your suicides never die of heart attacks. They choose easier ways out.

I called the police and the medical examiner and then sat back and had a nice hot cigarette. Who would ever believe my story? Ask yourself a question: without knowing the color of my skin, my religion, education, where I come from, or anything about me other than my name and address, is it possible to believe I had made a discovery that has an amazing power of putting a permanent end to all further wars by 1980, providing it is brought to light in time, but will also cause all other evils of human relations to decline and fail out of absolute necessity?

The death of Pretty Brilliant was hardly of such moment.

An hour passed in a minute or two and it was apparent the police weren't coming. Pretty soon the house began to stink like cat shit, and I felt as if all my friends in the world were telling me to drop dead.

Pretty Brilliant had died a lonely death. All death is lonely. History has recorded innumerable stories of a like nature, but is it necessary that the pattern continue?

I dialed my old friend Ralph Royster to ask about the retainer; he was out to lunch. I would drive over and pay him a call in person.

Royster lived in a distant part of the city that was deserted. All of its inhabitants except for the thieves and bullies had gone off elsewhere. We are never alone in that.

Every favor asked is a form of advance blame. It is a matter of an eye for an eye. Resentment must follow, as the night follows the day. Suppose you asked me what time it is, which is plainly saying—"Do me a favor, look at your watch, and tell me the time." Now supposing I ignored this, would you say, "Didn't you hear me?" And if still ignored, you might walk away calling me some kind of nut.

So it was with me and Royster. He was always referring clients to me, and they were usually quite dead. I never could get over resenting him for that. Yet he was said to be my very closest male friend. Asking favors, and telling each other what to do, is responsible for more divorces, adultery, disrespect, and hate, than you could ever dream was possible . . .

The Royster household seemed small. There had once been two live children, possibly even four, by my sister Pauleen, but now there was only Ralph, a pretty crazy guy in the old days, and the rather lovely French maid, Rio Rita. She let me in through the front door when the overhead light went out.

GET THE HELL IN HERE, said my old friend, greeting me in his pajamas from the anteroom to the main parlor. He was mixing a salad with his hands. From his day of hard labor in the garden he looked pretty worn and tired. The pretty maid, Rio Rita, went off, meanwhile, to fix up a stew.

It was getting late. A fireplace blazed. I thought we probably needed more light. When you consider the Boer War, World War I, Vietnam, you sometimes wonder about certain men.

After a moment Ralph interrupted his salad-making to glance at me with his impish little grin. YOU KNOW SOMETHING, MARTIN, he said, I'LL BET ANYTHING YOU'VE COME HERE TO TELL ME ABOUT PRETTY BRILLIANT DYING AND I DO NOT HAPPEN TO BELIEVE IT.

NEEDLESS TO SAY, he added with a grunt, I DIDN'T DO ANYTHING.

"I never said you did. To the best of my knowledge it was murder . . ."

Royster added more salt.

"There weren't any clues," I told him. "Not even mutilation . . ."

Royster smirked. "You can hardly blame anybody for that . . ."

Just then the maid interrupted us. She had urgent business with Ralph in the kitchen downstairs.

When he came back up again he was a very different person, and so was I. Are we supposed to condone murder, rape, war, and the wholesale slaughter of six million Jews? The hair stood up on my arms like a cat ready to fight.

Ralph said, "My will is not my own. I'm not free . . ."

"Consequently," I put in, "since B is an impossible choice when compared to A, man is not free to choose A . . ."

Ralph looked at me somewhat sternly: TURN THE OTHER CHEEK . . .

And when I did, he kicked me swiftly in the ass, and said, THOU SHALT NOT BLAME.

"It's sort of my bread and butter," I explained, BEING A PRIVATE DICK.

"I'm sorry," he said, "I couldn't help myself really, since my will is not free."

We had shed the last stage of that rocket that had given us all our thrust up to that point.

GO ON BACK TO PRETTY BRILLIANT, Ralph

said. FIND THE MURDERER AND SET HIM FREE.

I DON'T QUITE SEE WHAT YOU MEAN . . .

THE TRUTH, Ralph explained, THE TRUTH SHALL SET US FREE.

I went back to the apartment of Pretty Brilliant and let myself in through the front door.

She had disappeared, corpse and all.

Just then the phone rang.

Luckily it was the police.

I WANT TO REPORT A MISSING CORPSE, I told them.

STAY RIGHT WHERE YOU ARE, they said, AND WE'LL BE RIGHT OVER.

I let myself out quickly through the front door.

A crowd had assembled in haste. The way they looked at me they seemed to think I was the assassin.

I shall now demonstrate what could be called a virtual miracle, but remember, since my will is not free, it is impossible for me to take credit for it.

The father is weeping bitterly over the death of his loved one. The people standing around are shocked over the sight. Nobody can produce the corpse.

An ambulance arrives to carry off Pretty Brilliant, and tow trucks to pull the ambulance. Roberta Flack slowly sings, THE FIRST TIME EVER I SAW YOUR FACE.

The sun stands out on the face of the moon.

Pretty soon my old friend Ralph Royster arrives. There are tears in his eyes. He looks ugly, homely, stupid, dumb, coarse, bloated, unintelligent, and uneducated. Rio Rita has left him for developing a sexual habit.

"This would not have happened," he said, "had they lent me the money . . ."

You can lead a horse to water, but you can't make him drink.

If MAN is not responsible for his crimes, who is?

Ralph was saying, "This might not have happened . . . never . . ."

I said I agreed for the sake of the dead who are not presently with us.

The two survivors picked themselves off the ground, and both knew that no one would be coming along to blame them for this horrible tragedy.

Abruptly Royster spit in my face.

TURN THE OTHER CHEEK, I told him, and kicked him right in the ass.

A FRIEND'S STORY

The following story was told to me by my old friend David Archer, the architect.

He was in the country for a weekend, not too far from his mother's house in Wispride.

He was pruning a fruit tree on his front lawn.

The telephone rang on the sun porch.

He went inside the house on the fourth ring and said, "Hello, Archer residence."

A woman said, "This is the Department of Social Services calling, and we have a very nice young man who needs a room . . ."

He said, "You must have the wrong number."

He hung up and went back outside, never giving the call another thought.

The next day was Sunday.

He was reading the *Book Review* over his second cup of coffee on the back lawn.

The front door bell rang.

Nobody else was at home. He interrupted his comfort to get up, open the back door, and go through the house to the front door, which he opened also.

A very nice young man was standing on the stoop carrying a rather large battered-looking suitcase.

Archer said, "Hello . . ."

"I was sent by the Department of Social Services," said the very nice young man, with a very nice smile on his face as he spoke, so that, at first, my friend Archer was startled and did not know how to respond.

Then he remembered this must be the wrong number.

Archer said, "I think there has been some mistake . . ."

"I had thought so too," said the young man, "until I saw your face . . ."

"What about my face?" asked Archer.

"It's very nice," said the young man, "if you don't mind my saying so . . ."

"On the contrary," my friend said. "I feel the same about you.

"But," he went on, after a rather longish pause, "there must be some mistake because I don't happen to rent rooms. I told the people on the phone that . . ."

"I know." The young man did not seem put off.

Archer asked, "You came anyway?"

"When you said wrong number," the young man said very clearly, "I knew you meant the wrong number. I'm afraid you have the wrong number. Something like that. I was listening very carefully so I heard it very clearly. That is not quite the same thing as saying you had no rooms to rent. Do you live here all alone?"

"On weekends I do, generally speaking," said Archer, who was rather taken aback by so much careful familiarity. "Why do you ask?"

"To know."

"Know what?"

"That you live alone because you have no family . . ."

"Very true but I have a few friends . . ."

". . . In the city?"

"Yes . . . that too. What difference does it make when I've already told you I don't rent rooms?"

"But you could if you wanted to . . ."

"I suppose so, yes . . ."

"Couldn't you please," the young man pleaded, "make an exception for me just this once?"

"I'm afraid not!"

Archer was beginning to think less and less of this young man's face. In fact, he was about to slam his door on it. A man's home, after all, is his castle, or should be.

With or without their nice faces he really didn't like strangers.

Again he repeated, "There must be some mistake, and there is. I distinctly remember giving the impression I was not in the least bit interested in renting a room to anybody . . ."

"The impression, yes, you did do that surely, but we thought you were merely playing hard to get . . ."

"And that's why you came all the way out here?"

"It wasn't that far, and besides," he added, brightening suddenly, "I wanted to see if you had a nice face . . ."

Archer was outraged, or, at very least, as he told me later, blushing.

He slammed the door and went back to his papers on the back lawn.

A few minutes later the phone rang again.

He was tempted not to answer, but when the ringing persisted did as he had done previously, only going to the phone this time rather than to the front door.

"Hello," he said again, "Archer residence . . ."

"And thank goodness," said a woman's not unfamiliar voice, "because we've been ringing you forever . . ."

"What can I do for you now?" asked Archer.

"This is the Department of Social Services again, as you very well know, and you have a very nice young man with a very nice young face waiting at your front door . . ."

"What does he want from me?"

"A room . . ."

"I already told you you had the wrong number," said Archer. "I don't happen to rent rooms here. This is someplace where I go to get away . . ."

"Then may we try you in the city?"

"I'm afraid not." Archer was by now getting a bit giggly, as if so mildly irritated that it was almost like amusement. He said, "My apartment there is very small . . ."

"Then what shall we do with the young man with the nice face?"

Archer said, "He isn't my problem . . ."

"He's everybody's problem," went the voice, "and he's been waiting on your front stoop now almost an hour . . ."

"But I never said I would help . . ."

"We thought you were probably just shy . . ."

"Look," said Archer, "I haven't got the time or the patience for this kind of business . . ."

"If you feel that way about it you don't have to charge anything. We'll call it your contribution. The young man will be very pleased . . ."

"Not on your life," cried Archer. "I don't want to have anything to do with this."

"I understand . . ."

"You do?" He was beginning to feel somewhat guilty. "Precisely what do you understand?" he demanded.

"That you are unfriendly . . ."

"Yes."

Archer asked, "And now you won't be bothering me anymore?"

"Certainly not. You just go and tell the young man he is to return to the Department of Social Services because you're much too selfish . . ."

"That isn't fair . . ."

"Mr. Archer, we can't leave a perfectly nice young man like that standing outside your door all night long . . ."

"I never even invited him here."

"That," said the voice, firmly, "is your problem, Mister."

There was such silence then, my friend felt he would somehow be compelled to do as he was told, if he did not immediately speak up and protest.

Groping for something more to say, he asked, "What's his name?"

"Whose name?"

"Your young man's."

"*Our* young man's," said the voice, as if pleased to note Archer's interest.

"Cut it out. What's his name?" Archer insisted. "Never mind the rest . . ."

The voice said, "Be right with you . . ."

Archer could hear the flippity-flappity of a Wheeldex card file and then, "Yes here it is . . . Hello. Are you there?"

"Yes . . ."

"The name is Wurry . . . Stephen Wurry, according to our records, and it says here he is a very nice young man. Extremely. You'll be pleased to meet him, I'm sure . . ."

"I already have, and I have no intention . . ."

"Then won't you say good-bye to Mr. Wurry for us," went the voice, "and send him back to us where he belongs so we can find him another place . . ."

"Don't you worry," went Archer. "I will do just that!"

He hung up, and went out through the back door, and around the side of the house alongside his rose trellis to the front door.

There stood Wurry, suitcase in hand, his nice young face looking just a little drawn. Noticing Archer he asked, "Are you still looking for somebody?"

"I have a message for you," my friend said, "from the Department of Social Services . . ."

"Yes indeed?" Wurry seemed rather amused. He was grinning slyly, as if only out of certain strict corners of his mouth.

"You are to return to the Department," Archer said, "and they will find you another place. I'm afraid I was right all along and there has been some mistake. I'm sorry if you were inconvenienced . . ."

"I am too, Mister, believe me."

The young man didn't budge.

At last Archer said, "What are you waiting for now?"

"They're always making mistakes," the young man said. "How do I know they're not right this time? It certainly feels right to me . . ."

Archer asked, "You are Mr. Wurry?"

"Yes of course I am . . ."

"Then there is no mistake about the fact that there has been a mistake made. I just spoke to the Department and they agreed . . ."

". . . As far as you and they were concerned," went the young man, "but what about me? Nobody bothers to ask me what I think."

"Look here, you don't want to stay where you're not wanted, do you?"

"Maybe you just think you don't want me," said the young man. "Maybe if you got to know me better you'd like me a whole lot more . . ."

Archer felt that he must settle the matter once and forever.

"Frankly," he said, "I doubt that awfully much. But even if I did not I don't have the time to take on the mistakes of others. Now will you please go . . ."

"Well all right, if that's the way you feel about it." But nice young Mr. Wurry did seem somewhat downcast.

He picked up his suitcase and started walking away, then at the front hedge turned and faced Archer again, wearing a somewhat sheepish look.

"I suppose," he said, "if I were a beautiful young girl it would be different with you . . ."

"I wouldn't be too sure of that," said Archer.

"I suppose not," went the young man. He nodded his head sadly again and spat once into the bushes, as if for good luck.

The next day, upon returning to the city, Archer called the rural telephone exchange to which he belonged and had the number on his country house altered from 87405 to 84735.

He felt very sure that he had made the right decision, and just to make certain did not go to the country again for the next three weekends.

On the fourth weekend he was feeling very lonely and went off. He arrived in time to see the first crocus peering up through his lawn, and no sooner had he opened the front door to his house when the phone bell crackled in the musty atmosphere.

"If this is the Department of Social Services," asked Archer, when he had picked up at last, "how did you get my new number?"

"Very simple," went the same voice he had heard twice before with so much despair. "We called the telephone company."

"Now what do you want from me?" Archer demanded.

"Very simple," the voice again replied, "we just haven't got any nice pretty young girls who want to live with you . . ."

"I never asked you to . . ."

". . . You would if you could," went the voice. "Sorry. The next best thing is to choose a man . . ."

"A nice young man, I suppose?"

"Yes, of course," went the voice, "a nice young man with a nice young face would be very nice, we think, don't you?"

"But supposing I don't want anybody . . . at all . . . Supposing I prefer to be all alone . . . like now . . ."

"We already knew that," went the voice. "We've all known that all along and that's why we've all been trying to help."

AND, asked Archer, loudly and coarsely, HAVE YOU GOT ANYBODY IN MIND?

"Certainly not Wurry. He wouldn't do at all. Besides he's already found his place . . ."

"I'm sorry to hear that," went Archer. "I mean glad . . ."

"Sorry will do. Look," said the voice, "why don't you come downtown and we'll talk about it. You'll fill out some forms and talk to one of our people and perhaps we can help to find you a place."

"Nonsense! I already have a place for myself . . . two, in fact . . ."

"Stupid of me, of course, Mr. Archer. You're Mr. Archer, and you're not looking to live somewhere but to rent out rooms. Am I correct?"

"I . . . I guess so . . ."

"Then I'll just have to call you back . . ."

Five minutes later the phone rang again, and again, and again.

When Archer went to pick up he was greeted by another nice young man's voice.

"*Hello . . . ?*"

"*Hello . . . ?*"

"Are you Mr. Archer, the person who wants to rent a room in his private country house to a perfect stranger provided he is a male . . . ?"

"I suppose so," said Archer, who was by now just a little bit addled.

"Are you quite sure, because you don't want somebody to make the trip all the way out there for nothing."

Archer was growing rather excited.

"Yes I think so, I'm sure . . . Quite . . . ," he said at last. "I'm positive."

FAGG CRETIN SISSY, went the voice. STAY RIGHT WHERE YOU ARE AND I'LL BE RIGHT OVER.

THE BUFFALO HUNTER
as Told to Richard Elman

"Buffalo hunting has gone out of fashion over the last sixty years or so, and I'm not so sure I know why. Myself, I love those great fat beasts for the fierce bushy-coated monsters they really are. About the rights or wrongs of their former treatment I have no sentimental views whatsoever.

"That's for the past to judge and decide. Add to this the fact that most of my work nowadays has been in what I would call the Greater New York area, and you'll know why those of us who are still in the game think we are in a depressed industry. It's hard to make any sort of a real living anymore hunting bulls inland, or on either coast, especially this one, and sometimes you feel lucky when you get a crack at some old droopy teated cow in the Syracuse Public Gardens. Most of the best bulls are also stuck in zoos, too, and that's pretty much off the beaten track for most old scouts unless you happen to be the sort of person for whom it's real important, like myself. I'd hunt buffalo any day in the week, for the sport, but also because I truly believe somebody has to, if you know what I mean.

"I'm a man and I know the kind of things a man must do. Wandering across our plains under a sort of benign federal protection are herds of these great black bison. Even more depressing than the fate of such overprotected minions is the dwindling demand for their skins and hooves. All that delicious saline flesh lying out under the sun to ripen is get-

52

ting to be just plain rotten. The little meat I have to sell nowadays usually is tough and stringy, sort of like a pot roast. I don't do it for the money I make, which is minimal, but so I can stand on my own two feet like a man and say I am a man. Give me a good strong hearty buffalo bull any day in the week and he'll go down on you fast and hard, in a tumble of legs and dust, but only if one is a crack shot.

"I began my hunting escapades when I was only four years old in Wyoming near a town called Gillette, where I was born. Pa had me fitted out with a long bore Winchester with a special Zeiss sight that was his before it was ever mine. Before me Pa was a buffalo hunter, too, and his father also, before him, I think. It was just important to them to keep these family traditions alive. When the herds in our neighborhood were all played out Pa gave me permission to work the area around Helena, Montana, and later, as I say, I came East to specialize in zoos, and circuses, and public exhibitions.

"I've been knocking around a lot since then. I'm not really choosy where I go. Once a buffalo walks across my sights I just squeeze that trigger.

"I'm proud to say, though, I have never killed a buffalo in anger any more than I would knowingly strike a child.

"In 1921 when I was seventeen I had wandered off by myself as far south as the Grand Tetons in pursuit of fresh buffalo meat. The attrition to the herds was great, I'm sorry to say, and what refrigeration we could provide ourselves with was mostly cumbersome, expensive, and impractical. Remote though it was, I followed after them, killing what I could and slicing the viands into lumps and pieces that I stowed inside rawhide sacks, or baggies, leaving the remains for the vultures who hovered overhead always.

"I'm proud to say I fed more than my share of those awful birds.

"I was a strapping lad, brawny and strong, and, some people said, handsome. Sometimes more than twice my weight in buffalo meat was mine for the toting, not to mention the curly-headed skins of these great beasts that make such excellent sleeping robes.

"In those barely settled parts of the West door-to-door salesmanship of buffalo meat by horse was a novelty. I sold chops, flanks, and rumps. I packed the meats in salt and vinegar grass. I sold the ivories for bone-handled knives. But large numbers of my target population were presently so decimated that I had to remove myself to one of the few reserves then in operation to kill to order.

"I'm real proud to say I did all this in a businesslike way too, it never being my intention to profiteer off the miseries of either the homesteaders, or their herds, but to provide fresh-killed provender at a price all could afford.

"Nowadays there is little real demand for my pemmicans except in certain bars in places like Grand Junction and Norfolk, Nebraska. Too often I have locked a great beast into my sights who then had to be let scot free for fear of spoilage.

"You know, it's not as if we don't manage to waste a whole lot of other things in this country. I often wonder why are we suddenly so hotsy-totsy pollyannaish about the herds.

"Certainly it seems like hypocrisy to me that one fine day you can get people all hepped up about killing and then some people go soft-hearted and it's naughty naughty if you even try to pull one by the tail.

"How I got the idea of shooting at the ones that were locked up back East inside cages or behind palisades was, I thought to myself one fine day, if all the buffalo in the world are dead and gone forever where will that leave me with time on my hands to kill? But on the other hand, until that day comes along don't give me all this fancy sweet talk about conservation because I must get what is mine and you must get what is yours and we are not doing a single buffalo any favors by treating them so soft. Growing fat and lazy off salt peanuts and crackerjacks never really seems to help anybody.

"I'm not trying to excuse violence. Things might be very different if we were all still wild, or could be made to feel a bit more useful to each other, once in awhile.

"My last big kill was in the winter of '63 near Rimouski, Quebec, Canada: a smallish circus with an imitation Bill Cody act in which the old guy was played by some Italian faggot from Calgary, not to mention the gal who played Annie Oakley doubling as the bearded lady.

Well, suddenly there was three of these great big boogers just there to be had for the asking, and I lined them up in my sights so I could split a red cunt hair and went *rat tat tat* just once with a burst of my Italian Beretta grease gun from maybe sixty feet away.

"That lead bull was large, and albinoish along the haunches. He sort of rolled right over and died, giving me one of those looks which you sometimes get from dying critters, when it only goes to prove, I guess, that they have their feelings just like the rest of us.

"Since then my life has been a series of random pot shots scattered about here and there, in Brooklyn, the Bronx, the Catskill game farm up near Kingston, and, oh yes, another place in Oneonta, off some unpaved two lane highway, so that I sometimes wonder why do I bother?

"All my life I have been opposed to government charity, and I never could stand to see anybody leading the life of Riley.

"But what business is it of mine if a few old buffalo are getting off easy?

"There must be some as have earned the right to their old age, and a little leisure now and then, and this is, after all, a free country.

"Maybe it's because I believe in Freedom so strongly that I do the things I do. I mean, when our forefathers first came to these shores there were buffalo sufficient for ourselves and the Indians. Then people started getting greedy until somebody had to say who knew better, HOLD IT A MINUTE!

"Well, that's been going on now for as long as I can remember and nobody seems any less greedy. Meantime, what with people losing their taste for the meat, what are we going to do with all these unwanted buffalo?

"Now I say if it makes me feel good to stand on my

own two legs and kill a big old bull every once in a while like a man I don't really know who it's hurting except maybe a bunch of dumb old beasts who have been caged so long they don't know any better, and even when I run across a situation like that I always try to play fair and give the critters a fighting chance. For example, before I will fire a single shot I will try to get them to panic so they will be in motion and not just a bunch of sitting ducks. Also, I will never permit myself to kill a cow when she is nursing.

"Now you can say what you like: how do we know you're telling the truth, or you may act responsibly but what about others? But what I say is out West—from what I hear tell—they are losing folks again while the buffalo are once again thriving.

"Well, what I say is, who built up this great country to what it is today—people or buffalo?"

GOLDY

Getting to know those three bears real well was important to me. When I look back on my childhood those were the days I remember best of all. We were inseparables. The family I'd never really had were also my first real close friends. To this day I get a sort of lump in my throat whenever I eat cold porridge.

The big bears were just like a mother and father to me, and between Baby Bear and myself there grew up something thick, and close, and warm. He was like a little brother, my first and best friend. The fact that we were of such different sexes never seemed to matter. We played together all the time real nice, as friends and equals.

It is many years ago since that happened and when I went back to Grandma's house afterward I was never really very happy. It was a matter of totally different life-styles. We just couldn't relate as people any longer. Living all alone, in a cabin in the woods, with Grandma, was different from being with the bears. I lacked a playmate. The absence of real close family life was also a strain. Alone with myself a lot of the time, I had bad feelings. I came to think of myself as abandoned, neglected, a sort of waif. I developed a very slight squint.

It had to be so, for the bears had all moved on elsewhere, and Grandma, who had meant to be sweet, was at an age when tending to the needs of a small child like myself sapped nearly all of her energies. There was, in truth, very little real contact between us. It came out in therapy I re-

sented her for intruding on me by bringing me back home
again, and she, though probably meaning to be affectionate,
kept me at a certain distance, as if still fearful of me for the
life I was trying to lead.

Wringing her hands, she used to say, "If only your
parents were still living. It's so sad. So sad, *so sad*, O Goldilocks, I tell you it's just plain sad . . ."

"What is, Grandma?"

"You were such a beautiful child, and now look at you.
Look what's happening to you," and she would shrug, before breaking down into weeping tears again.

Mealtimes were especially painful for us. I had ac-
quired the habits of a vegetarian. The taste of Grandma's
delicious soups and stews, over which she labored so long, I
found repulsive. Once you have made real friends with an
animal it is apt to be that way with a person. But whenever I
asked for dairy, or something plain, like nuts and honey,
Grandma lost her temper.

"You're thin as a rail already," she would say, "and no
wonder. You never eat and though you say you want dairy
you don't drink any milk, and I wish you would try to cut
your fingernails . . ."

My fingernails were growing, and I was growing too.
Soon I was ten. Grandma bought the big old house in town
on South Front Street near the abandoned Grand Union,
and shortly thereafter I was sent off for my first day of
school.

Grandma had washed and ironed a very pretty dress
for me to wear. It was pink, made out of tufted organdy,

and it had little puffy short sleeves, and a widish sort of hem in imitation white lace.

Because there were all the scratch marks still on my arms, I refused to wear it. I preferred my old jeans and a polo.

"Don't be silly," she said. "They'll know anyhow. You've got a reputation . . ."

"So what?"

"So why not dress up," she said, "really put your best foot forward. That way you'll make friends with all the right people in town a whole lot easier."

She handed me my new patent-leather mary janes.

"Supposing I don't want to . . ."

"Stop talking like a tomboy," Grandma said, as she handed me the lunch box.

Dressed up as I was that first day, Little Red Riding-hood was just somebody I met during recess over milk and cookies to whom I was attracted immediately, as one girl to another, because we seemed, at first, to have a lot in common.

I mean she was just so fem and pretty, really and truly, just so vivacious, I suppose you could call it, and cute. She had this wonderful red hair in bunches across her shoulders, a really great imagination, and a pretty nice personality, too, and she told the wildest stories. Also, like me, she lived with her grandma.

We became best friends. We were both pretty lonely for company, and both liked animals and little-girl things, though the latter always seemed much more interesting to her.

At first we exchanged toys, and sleepover dates. Later we shared certain of our dolls, and pets. Red's grandma was called Ida. I always thought that was pretty far advanced to call your grandma Ida. I guess you might say I was impressed that they could seem so spontaneous together. They had a pretty little gingerbread-style house in Rosalba where I spent three of my nicest vacations.

At fourteen a lot of changes are taking place in girls and that's when we started dating, and even double-dating. Red's father had remarried, to a French woman, and he sent her a regular allowance. She had a lot of things I didn't have, but I had some things she didn't have, like my own social worker. The school had insisted on that.

My first real boyfriend was sandy-haired and cheerful. His name was Jake Crouch, which was also my social worker's first name, and he played touch football.

Jake liked me a lot. I always thought he liked Red even more, but she never even gave him a second glance.

All the boys in school were turned on to Red like that. She was just extremely popular in her standoffish sort of way because she was so very beautiful and girly, with all that red hair and all, and though she seemed to enjoy the admiration, she usually left everybody waiting around in line for nothing, like a bunch of suckers.

Even though she really wasn't very nice to them the guys never seemed to mind her numbers. I guess she'd had a pretty awful thing happen when she was a kid because she never seemed to know how to be with the rest of the gang at the drive-in and, you know, places like that. Even in junior high, Red wore nail polish and was already dating college boys.

That was really pretty peculiar since she'd told me once she really didn't like putting out that much. "I just can't stand being pawed all over like that," Red said. Looking at me she actually shuddered, like somebody with real cold hands had touched her all of a sudden in a sensitive spot.

I remember her shudder. It almost made me shudder. Poor thing, despite the fact she was so pretty and could seem so flirty, Red was just pretty sensitive and she had a real hard time of it in our high school.

It was sort of different with me. Since I knew I wasn't that beautiful I could be a lot more aggressive. All these loving feelings inside of me just had to come out, and besides, I liked boys. The guys used to say, "If you want to have a good time go with Goldilocks and keep Red Ridinghood's picture in your wallet."

Pretty soon Grandma said I was acting just like a slut.

Which really wasn't true at all, though I sometimes was pretty boy crazy. They made me feel so good all the time, like my insides were made of a hot jelly, and the way my nipples sometimes got so hot and tingly, too, I felt I wanted to do the same for them, if I just could.

At first all the guys were a little afraid of me because I was built pretty big for my age and looked sort of strong; and, since it was that awkward age for all of us, I had to wait my turn for the telephone calls, but after one or two dates I couldn't get rid of any of my new beaux. Now they were coming on to me as strongly as I had once come on to them, and sometimes I had a lot of homework to do. It was something I did with my lips, I guess.

Red Ridinghood, who was really just very very shy in ways I never was, I guess, had a study problem, too, just like me, but we were getting to spend less and less time together because we were just so competitive with one another it wasn't that easy for either of us. In home-room class, or gym, she was certainly the girl everybody looked at and mooned over, whereas, after a coke date with her, they were always coming around to see me for, if worst came to worst, a hand job.

I guess Red could get pretty jealous of me in that respect, too, because we never spoke about it except once, when I asked to borrow one of her long skirts for a date. Then she said, "You act as if you like boys better than anything else in the world."

She was wearing that new light pink shade of lipstick we'd seen together at McCrory's and pouting just a little.

Red said it was alright with her if I borrowed the skirt but I was not to let any boys go messing all over it with their stuff.

"Don't worry," I said. "You know I take good care of things. If anything like that seems even likely to happen I'll take the skirt off."

"Bet you won't be sorry to do that."

"What about you?" I replied. *"Would you be?"*

"Not really." She frowned.

The way things were between Red and myself it was getting harder and harder to have any fun even when we did spend the day together.

I don't know what happened to her. It happened to both of us. We just grew apart, is what I guess.

Almost as if she were afraid to remain a child for very much longer, Red had blossomed, suddenly and prematurely, into a blowsy fresh full-grown womanhood. It was like the real sudden heavy weight of white spring blossoms on a bare brown bough. At fifteen she was a 36 C, and had real nice long legs. She wouldn't baby sit with me anymore when I had to, and when I asked she sometimes looked cross. That adorable dimple on her chin was still prominent, but her eyes were black and deep, her skin milky white, her waist narrow, her hips wide, her thighs sleek and curved. She looked and acted so pretty, like a grown-up person, and sorta misty and sad all the time, and when she walked down the street sometimes the guys made funny noises behind her back.

I'm not saying the guys didn't find me cute too, but later when I looked in the mirror I always thought of myself as just plain dumpy, a bit too pushy and round, with maybe too much baby fat left on my frame. At least I wasn't such a hotsy-totsy like some people I know. Even when we were fooling around guys always thought of me as their pal. I was Honey, Goldy, Baby. They took me to hot movies, or ice skating, and let me turn on with them beneath the railway tracks. Nobody ever wrote me poems, or sent me flowers, except maybe for Peter Strul, and everybody in school knew he was a jerk.

The real bad time came when people started fucking in eleventh grade and just because I was so available all the boys were always coming around until I was practically out of my mind, and then I really got very angry at Red because she was getting all this admiration from practically every boy in school, and she really wasn't holding up her end of things at all. I mean I liked it, *okay, sure,* but I didn't like the looks I sometimes got from a lot of the other girls, particularly Red.

Once, after Driver Education, we were cycling home from school together. Along came Rip Jacobson on his Honda, and he really looked awful cute.

Red said, "He's awful cute that Rip. I suppose you let him do that with you too . . ."

I was off that day and Red knew it, and she was talking about the only boy in school I really liked doing it with. With Rip I really liked it a lot because he was always so tender.

I told Red, "It's different with Rip. It's special . . ."

"Why special?" Arching her beautiful brows, she asked, "What's so special about Rip . . . ?"

"To me he's just special," I told her. "With me he is, anyway . . . he's sweet . . ."

Rip had swung all the way around on his Honda and was cruising back past us again in the opposite direction.

I tinkled my little bell at him.

All of a sudden Red said, "Hi, Rip . . ."

He squeezed his hand brakes so hard he nearly fell over the handlebars.

"Well, hi," he said. "How are you?"

Pretty soon we were talking to each other, which meant they were, and making eyes, and turning all red in the face, as if I wasn't even there.

I got back onto my bike, and pedaled my way home as fast as I could, ran upstairs, threw myself across the bed, and cried.

I just felt like such a mess. It wasn't any fair. No fair at all. Red was always doing that sort of thing to me, and now she was going to take away Rip, too, when she really didn't even care for him. That was just her way of getting even with me about boys.

Well she wasn't coming to the party next week at Mary Poppoff's. I would make sure to talk to Mary and all the other girls we knew about that, and I would also speak to Rip and warn him not to make a fool of himself with that girl. I'd do it first thing tomorrow, after home-room class, if that wasn't too late.

Supposing they were already together. Just suppose they'd gone off together to Rip's finished basement with all the trophies on the wall, and he was doing that to her already while she was doing this to him . . .

Honestly, when I thought of them doing something like that together down there where we had been together so many other times you can believe me I was so furious I went right downstairs to the phone and called Red at home.

Ida answered.

No, Red wasn't home from school yet. Was there any message, Goldy?

TELL HER I HATE HER, I screamed. I NEVER WANT TO SPEAK TO HER AGAIN AS LONG AS I LIVE AND I HOPE SHE AND RIP ARE VERY HAPPY TOGETHER.

Then I went upstairs to the medicine cabinet and took the new razor which I had bought to shave under my arms and slashed both wrists and put them under cold water so that the blood kept running out until I was unconscious.

That's how I came to be here in the country again. It won't be forever because it can't. Nothing really is. I've learned that much. But nowadays, whenever I tell them what it felt like, the people here say, LIFE IS SAD, GOLDY. YOU HAVE TO TAKE THE GOOD WITH THE BAD. EVERYBODY HAS A LITTLE BIT OF HARD LUCK NOW AND THEN, AND YOU HAVE TO GROW UP AND FACE LIFE AGAIN AND BE STRONG AND SELF-RELIANT SO YOU CAN LEAVE THIS PLACE AND GO BACK OUT INTO THE WORLD AGAIN.

I'm really not too sure that's what I want just right now because I'm really not feeling very good about a whole lot of things.

The other day Grandma sent me a letter from that hunter who found me. He said the bears are back, but they are getting pretty old and weak and feeble, and Baby Bear just lost one of his front paws in a trap.

As far as my old chum Red is concerned, Grandma says she's getting married pretty soon, to a doctor.

PART 2

PLAYING WITH MARY

Mary was an artist. The most beautiful things she made look simple. She broke them apart, or built them up with her hands, played with them.

Mary was always trying to play. Surfaces attracted her. She joined them together so she could slip something of herself, a look or glance, between them, or beneath them. The love she bestowed on the world was playful. She was the child who jumped and squealed when the glass in the mirror rattled back at her fiercely.

If things or people wouldn't play she became angry, sulking. The experience had refused to be an adventure. She stayed inside herself all day, darkly.

The surface of her smooth face was always becoming a smile. Her hair was broken gold. When the color came to her cheeks she was beautiful. She broke out easily in hives. She hyperventilated, took too many different sorts of pills.

I loved Mary, I told her so, but she did not always love me. I was much too dark, too serious, and I refused to play. Did I even know what I wanted from her? She said she didn't. If we ever did come out to play together the pleasure would not be mutual.

Becoming Mary's friend was the gift she bestowed on those who were not her lovers. It wasn't always appreciated. I took what I could get. Mary seemed to need me. She never would say how, never named the need, though it was as certain as my need for her, to see her once in awhile at play. We encouraged each other, protected each other, crit-

71

icized each other; the rest between us was undefined. I was the person she had to report to when she was coming down from a giddy mood. She sometimes confused my sobriety for sanity, but only when she wasn't feeling well. She couldn't always be playful. Sometimes she said she wanted to see things more clearly.

Sometimes when Mary was soft and balmy she was being thoughtful. Love came on her again and again like drenching spring rains. She fell in love to be in love with the feeling; she'd loved me, more than once, I think; sooner or later she always told me about her other lovers. They were never very playful with her either. They got her down, or they got her high, or they brought her up short. Eventually she loved them all as one loves certain very cranky children. Mary seemed to think her mission was to make men more playful. She was always falling in love, then clouding over.

Of James Gibbon I knew only that he was considered "sexy," had once been a promising young composer, had a wife, three children, a talent. In our circle he had a crazed reputation. He was always crashing. He had driven himself crazy more than once. He was ambitious for the love of women. His music was said to need sweetening.

Mary met Jim at a party. They agreed to have lunch the next day. Afterward she took him home to see her rugs. On one of them they made love.

At the time I was away with a girlfriend in the woods. We were trying to disabuse ourselves of a long romance peacefully. It wasn't necessary to talk; we made love only to fill time. We thought we wanted to arrange all the future si-

lences between us. This going off together was like slowly
drawing the curtains closed again. If nothing else we would
have a certain drowsy peace with each other. I wrote a little,
swam a lot, painted, gardened. June allowed herself to do all
those domestic things which, at home in the city, she was
training herself not to feel guilty about neglecting. Sometimes for days we avoided being seductive with each other,
and when we came together then it was like the clap you
can make with a good old pair of sturdy mittens when you
bring them together.

Mary's letter arrived one day after a thundershower. It
was like a small stone thrown in through our window, left a
neat clean black hole in the day we had been so carefully
and tenderly rubbing up as bright again together.

"Hello again, luv, how are you? I'm in luv," she wrote,
as if her news should be as startling to me as it was to her. "I
don't think you know the fellow. You will. He needs to
meet new people. From what I've told him about you he
likes you very much. When do you expect to get back to
town? Can we have lunch?"

In her first paragraph Mary wasn't saying anything except to serve notice she might be getting a little tight about
her feelings for another person. Her second paragraph was a
rather lucid depiction of certain erotic delights. Afterward
Mary and Jim lay abed looking out a window; waves lapped
the shoreline below. There was a full yellow moon.

Mary's third paragraph was more or less an apology for
the intrusion.

"I gather you must be doing well you two up there

from all the accumulation of profound silence I have been gathering. Well, try to have fun and don't worry. I'll see you when you get back to the city. I'm really having a very good time here, luv. See ya . . ."

I made a special trip into town that evening to find a telephone and call Mary. She seemed very scared, scared enough to write, which was something she rarely did. I wondered about this new person. What about him was so attractive to Mary? I thought there might be a clue in that to something I was trying to write about myself. Chiefly I was concerned for my friend. She had never done herself any harm in the past with men except by worrying about them. I felt I detected in her good spirits a sort of despair, the doubt that she was responding fully and being responded to. With Mary I always considered myself empathic.

Our conversation was full of the shortcuts we had come to expect from each other.

"What fun Bob it's really you . . ."

She seemed breathless.

"Tell me who's the lucky fella . . . ?"

"Jim Gibbon you don't know him yet. He's a composer. You will . . ."

"Is he playful . . . ?"

Mary drew in her breath: "I'm really in love, Bob, and it's beautiful . . ."

I said, "You didn't answer my question."

"He's got a lot of problems," Mary said, as if warning me again, "but he can be very sweet. I think he's talented . . . I love being with him." She added abruptly: "*Why am*

I doing this? It's the sex. We're always making love . . ."

A sort of soft hurt. She had touched me in a sensitive spot. "Sounds to me," I told her softly, back, "like great fun. Maybe you ought to keep on trying . . ."

"Don't be mean to me," Mary teased. I could tell she was edging away from the contact she'd made. Surely Jim wasn't there with her now, or she would not have mentioned his problems. Mary was probably afraid of losing a certain hysterical edge on her mood, her spontaneity. She began to explain: "We're going away to the shore for a few days. I'm pretty nervous about that . . ."

I said, "You know how to have a good time. Will you be with other people?"

"I don't think so . . ."

"Mary," I said, "have fun and don't worry." But I felt I must contribute something of myself to the conversation if we were to talk at all.

"Listen, luv," I added, hastily, "June and I are breaking up and it's cool. Nice. I've never had that happen to me before."

"Don't let it get you down," Mary said. Our annoyance with each other was reduced to a nervous giggle. She said, "See you in the city. Got to rush now. Jim should be here any minute. I'm not even dressed . . ."

"Maybe you ought to stay that way," I teased. Mary was giggling me off the phone.

I came back to the woods looking haunted. June was angry with me at a glance. Why must you always punish yourself? Between Mary and me she could only sense a certain dim far-off possibility to be jealous over. It so happened she *was* jealous, and suspicious of me too; she seemed to know that whether Mary and I were ever lovers I cared much more for Mary than I did for her.

Troubled with gnats, her pretty face wore a vapid look. She sat at the edge of the pond, with her feet thrust into the water. After our initial exchange she did not look up to talk, but watched the spread of ripples, asked, "How's Mary?"

"I think she's having a pretty good time." Downcast too, I spoke rapidly at my shoes. "She really seems to be having herself a ball . . ."

"I already knew that and so did you," June said. She wanted to be spoken to. She didn't like our shortcuts. June was an angry, passionate girl. She was not at all playful like Mary. She spoke things flat out, and then drew closer, touched you. She could be warm, tender. With June you were always breaking through something together.

Now she was staring at me as if I was wasting her time.

"Mary thinks she's in love," I told June gravely.

"O . . . that . . . Poor Bob." She turned away from me and spat into the pond.

Later in bed we made it up with each other. She saw my concern for Mary was real, not condescending. She came to accept my story of need and fascination, and that it was not just a crush. "I don't know why you and Mary don't make love *anyway*," June volunteered. "I mean, after all, you've both tried just about everybody else."

We were laughing at each other with a sly ease. "I think you may be right about that," I teased. "Maybe we should, the sooner the better . . ."

Over breakfast in the morning June began to talk about when we might be getting back to the city.

It was early fall before I actually got to see Mary in person. Though we spoke on the phone more than once soon after my return, no personal invitations were ever made. Our conversations reverted to gossip about others. We were reconnoitering the distance between each new call and the last. Mary didn't seem to wish to show herself to me, and I was feeling about the same way. When she asked how things were with June and myself I didn't bother to return the compliment.

I wasn't that interested in the person I was now with; I might as well have been with June; it was at a party after a friend's opening that we saw each other at last in person.

Mary had come alone. Jim was supposed to be meeting her later. She looked pretty. To a person like Mary that look is not always becoming. Though I saw her first, she was the one who drew closer. She came up to me and before I knew it was holding my hand, rubbing up against me. She always did things like that with me at parties, and it never seemed to happen when we were alone. I told her glibly, "Hey, you know that's really nice, Mary."

When she moved away from me she was blushing. Her large blue eyes had been glistening. Now they went blank, cold. I knew she had seen Jim in the crowd.

Even before he began to move toward us I picked out

his face from the others. A narrow gaunt-looking man with a beard, a scar on his lower cheek next to his lips, lustrous dark eyes, a hollow look. My rival seemed to fit Mary's mood exactly. He was not very tall, I saw, as he came closer, but sort of slim and spry-looking. He wore a fitted denim work suit and gold-rimmed glasses, seemed at once cool and trim, with a crude hard sexual energy. His eyes were flitting from me to Mary but his glance rested on her, an open sensual look of want.

"*Hi* . . ."

"*Hi* . . ."

Jim took me in again: "So you're the person I've been hearing so much about . . ."

"The feeling is mutual . . ."

Mary said, "Let's all have a drink."

They hadn't kissed at first but now she threw herself at Jim and kissed him heavily on the cheek. He drew back and pulled her toward him and kissed her open-mouthed.

Mary broke away again. She took Jim's hand. She was leading him toward the bar. I started to follow them.

"Let's have two drinks if necessary," Mary said. "Let's all get drunk. Bob, where's your date?"

I shrugged. My date was across the room getting interested in a Movement type in a pea jacket. I pointed out her elegant slouch and blonde hair.

"Nice," Jim hissed. He was merely trying to seem admiring.

Mary said, "Why not bring her over and let's get introduced?"

"If you like . . . later . . ." I knew Mary was trying to be playful again to fill up the silence; she never got drunk, and if she wanted us all to be playful together that only meant she was willing to be negligent with me for Jim's sake and for my sake was unwilling to allow Jim to fix her in his stare. But, so that we both would not feel neglected, a fourth person was necessary, and almost any fourth person would do. Mary might have grabbed at the nearest shoulder, but she asked me to produce a date.

I finished my drinks quickly, shook Jim's hand, touched my lips to her cheek, and started away from them to corral Helen.

Mary broke away. She followed me. She caught me wandering near the door.

"You'll call me, won't you, we'll have lunch . . ."

I asked, "Why not make it dinner?"

Mary said, "Jim really liked you . . ."

"Did he tell you so?"

Her face looked as if it had been steamed over. She tried to recover from her disapproval by wetting her lips. I knew she wanted me to say something friendly to her about Jim, but since I was also supposed to be her critic I could see her preparing in back of all that a look that would anticipate wounds.

At last I said, "He's very handsome."

Mary said, "That's an insult . . ."

"He looks quite vigorous too." I smiled.

She was avid with me: "You stinker . . ."

"I love you," I said. "You know that . . ."

"You will call?"

"Whenever you like," I insisted, "or you call me . . . I love you," I repeated. But I was lying to myself. This wasn't really my mood. I didn't want to love Mary. I wanted her to recognize me. I was being playful with her. I wanted her more than I'd ever wanted any other woman then and there and it was all out anger.

I said, "Tell me one thing . . ."

"Yes, luv . . ."

My body was swelling and softening. I looked at her and reached out and took her deftly into my arms and kissed her lips and pressed her breasts and hips and released her with a touch of my tongue against her lips again.

"Mary," I said, "Mary . . . Come with me . . ."

"What is it dear?" she asked. "What's the matter?"

"Tell me something . . . You must . . ."

"Dear, what is it?"

"Why don't we ever make love?"

My voice was husky. Her soft red face seemed all wet. She said, "I really don't think that's the question . . ."

"Well, I do . . ."

"Yes," she blinked back. "I guess so too. I understand . . ."

"I want to be with you," I said.

"I understand . . ."

"So?" I was becoming impatient with her again.

Mary drew herself up but failed and went limp and soft again: "I'll try giving you a one-sentence answer . . ."

"Do, luv . . ."

"We're both busy getting to know other people . . ."

"So?"

"When you call we'll talk about that," Mary said, "I promise," as if she were making me some other sort of vague promise she intended to keep as vague if I did not release her immediately to Jim, whom she seemed to see out of a corner of one eye and was beckoning to come join us again.

Suddenly Mary saw me laughing and she was laughing with me, again easily.

Besides," she added suddenly, "you're always too busy. I doubt if you could ever fit me in . . ."

She was leaving me for her lover to play with me another time. I felt a sudden intense high glee, said, "I'll make room for you any time, Mary," and again I kissed her lightly just as Jim joined us.

"Well, call me," Mary said then.

"I will call . . . I'll call . . ."

Jim asked, "Are you two at it again?"

"You'll call me," I said, more loudly now. "*You'll call me* . . ."

"I promise I'll call." She was frantic. "Now go away please and I'll call." For how could she call if I wouldn't go away?

My date had noticed us. She was standing pat, staying clear. Jim looked as if he might boil over at any minute. Mary's look was not pleading; it was more or less the excuse she gave for not being able to.

"Mary darling," I told her, "either you call me tomorrow or I'll call you . . ."

She smirked.

"That's enough, you two," Jim said. He tried to laugh.

"Goodnight, you two," I said. I was laughing.

I went across the room again. I felt very sexy. I was being watched. My face was ablaze. I was really giggling out loud. I thought I was going to be very happy someday and make somebody very happy, if not Mary then somebody else. At that moment every woman in the room was Mary and I thought they all wanted to play with me.

THE FLIRT

I admired him so much I was afraid of him. I think he was beautiful the way he looked, all sparkly. Such brilliant eyes, dark skin, curly thick black hair. Sometimes his lips pouted. He was trying to be the person he was not. A happy person. My questioning glances sometimes angered him. I thought I could see his other face. If he knew me too, he was going to let that knowledge be. I wanted to be close, closer than we were. We could try to keep each other happy. I loved him.

At the pool I loved staring at his body. He was so slim. The body of a Greek boy. He looked like one of the figures on those vases. I wanted to touch him. I thought if I touched his face I would see him and know him, again and again. More and more I felt love for him. He was so beautiful. It seemed not at all apparent to him.

I knew he wanted to be my friend, though at a distance. Because I loved him I was afraid. Suppose we ever touched. From a little way off he was so wonderful to look at, so different whenever we drew closer. He always made me feel like smiling. He had drawn himself into a deep careless slouch. He could not keep himself forever strict and featureless. His lithe serene looks had been daubed over with a crackled glaze.

L seemed determined to avoid me by becoming my guardian. I ministered to the hurt with flattery; sometimes I asked his advice: about my life, the trips I wanted to take, other people. His voice could be so soft, and soothing. "You must do what you want to do," he said once, smiling at me, gently, almost indifferently. "I believe the experience you put off is the experience you will never have . . ."

Sometimes I was afraid of his indifference. Was it contempt? What did he hide? He would see more of me than he cared to show of himself. We were both in this place for the same reasons. Life had frightened us very much. Why did he always pretend he was not afraid? His indolent grace was beautiful, but meaningless to me. With all of us he behaved like a trustee. He would be listening to our chatter; soft-eyed, he would drift away into himself again. I felt I wanted to arrest that drift, to seize him and hold him close in time. We could make love. What if he didn't like me after that . . . ?

I was not afraid he would call me names. It was evident to me he was a man who had loved other men like that. His pouting look always seemed to be saying so. But he would never openly declare himself. He offered us no certainties. Why? His smile was always sudden, unexpected; it could make him seem so grave. What was he up to? What did he want except this fine certitude of distance between us? He would never say, and I was never that sure of myself to ask. I didn't like experimenting with the feelings of others. I thought I knew how I felt. I wondered how he really felt. To be that close, his friend or lover, just to know him, frightened me. Getting any closer to him would be almost like responding to a dare.

One day I sent him a note: "They tell me now I can leave here whenever I feel like it. *You too . . . ?* I'm trying

to make plans. If you'd like to take a trip to Greece with me
I might be interested . . ."

The feeling was choked in L's politeness. Wishing to
avoid being flirtatious I was not quite direct. I think I knew
what to expect. Somehow, no matter what he might say to
me now, my enthusiasm for the trip would be diminished. I
was convinced the fault was as much mine as his.

But for a day or so I didn't hear from L at all. As if he
hadn't ever read my words, he just continued to look at me,
quietly, over the dinner table, and his smile remained nice,
easy, a sort of bestowed benevolence. On the second day
after lunch he stopped me as I was going to my room. His
hand held me easily. I knew the smell of his breath. "I'm
going away for a few days to see a friend."

I was afraid. He would be leaving before me. Perhaps
he would never be coming back.

While he was gone I went with others. I was so determined not to be alone I had a love affair. I would wait. My
sort of protection was to find myself a woman. I felt he had
left me so naked to myself, and the others. I needed to hide
out with somebody for awhile.

She was very beautiful and she excited me. With her I
struggled to retrieve the space in my life he had vacated.
With our eyes open we made love until she swore she was
in love with me. Again and again I responded to her words.
They were almost like feelings. I was surprised I could be so
tender with her. I felt so much going on inside me I called it
love.

Late at night we would make love. She always woke me early in the morning with her hands to make love to her again. We talked a lot in soliloquies. Whenever I stared into space she pawed at me. Sometimes I think I knew her better than anybody I have ever known. I was in love with my knowledge of her. I made her tell me everything.

The sprawled splendors of her body sometimes frightened me. Reaching her had been this sudden act. I was always about to flee; really I didn't wish to avoid myself with her. To become the person I wanted to be I needed to be myself. I was suspicious, impatient. Since she seemed to want to hold me to our passion I demanded she tell me more and more about herself. I had to know her even more, so well that I could be with her at last, or reject her. I distrusted all the tenderness I was feeling. She was *here, with me* in this place; I thought she must be like me, too.

I began to feel sorry for her. These moments of pity disgusted me. Except when making love I was secretive, silent, withdrawn. She would know me best, I told her, by not hiding anything from me. She was open with me then and I was pitiless. I loved her tenderly, ruthlessly. I said afterward, "I'm in love." I did not say who the person was.

Once she was so completely with me I told her I loved her. I was very lonely that night. All the time L was away. The incompleteness I felt was that something might happen between us while he was away and I would not know what it meant beyond the feeling.

When we were almost sleeping she spoke my name. She spoke to me like a woman. She said she wanted me again. She said she loved me. I held her very close. The moment passed.

Later she woke me. There were certain things she still had to tell me. I must listen.

I was barely awake. Her excitement with me seemed almost sinister. She was pawing at my flesh so that I felt it would come loose in strips. I tried to find my feelings. I was too groggy. Listening to her voice had made me drowsy.

She told me she had lied to me. Before this she had never known such happiness. Her marriage had never been happy; her husband was frightened of her. The lovers she had known had *always* been the same: distant, cold, unhappy people. She wanted to live now but so much sudden pleasure always made her remember her past. She said she knew me. If there was somebody else in my life, she didn't care.

She told me of meeting Alice B. Toklas in Paris during her honeymoon. Her husband had taken her to meet Miss Toklas and for a little while they had all been very gay together. Miss Toklas told her she was beautiful, and fresh to look at. She said she had not been so happy again for a long long time. Always she wanted me to remember that. She said she hoped we could see each other even after we were released. She told me she was sure she loved me. She said she wanted to spend all her remaining time with me. She said her real life began the day we met.

When I left her I felt very lonely and so full of the strangest feelings. I thought I must be in love.

L was expected back the next day. When I awoke my

body felt large, porous. I thought for him I was being so open we would probably become lovers. Certainly I would see him again today.

After breakfast I waited on the porch in sunny summer dust to greet him. Then I went to the art cabin and waited for him to come to me through one of those golden spaces between the aisles of elms. I returned to the porch after lunch to wait for him again.

L passed by briefly at three. I knew he was not trying to look for me. That would not be like him. He would always want to seem pleasant, cool, well-mannered, distant. For me to know that he was aware of me without forcing me to commit myself. He went by waving his hand. I was to assume he knew we must talk later.

Again at dusk in the downward afterglow of light from the altar window in the hall I came upon him standing with his back to me to read mail, his glossy black hair all radiant. At the sound of my footfall his movement was sudden, tensile. He knew it was me approaching; he called out my name.

I came even closer to say his name.

Abruptly he turned and we were smiling. I told him I was so glad he was back. He said he felt the same way. He seemed just glad to be with me again. More so than he would permit himself to say.

I asked about his trip.

L told me he was exhausted. He had gotten very little sleep the night before.

I was afraid to ask anything at all about his friend. L was waiting for me to speak. At last I told him he should probably rest. We would talk later.

"I'll be happy to see you later," he said, "any time . . ." His face seemed a bit wan. He was trying hard again to seem gentle with me, and even. He whispered at me, "Thank you . . ."

The woman knew what was happening to us now because she had seen L and me together. Her passion for me only increased. She wanted me to come to her room, and I went.

At dinner later I sat alone. Afterward in the hall L again approached. He asked if I had given any thought to our trip while he had been away.

I felt he must be teasing me. I wanted him to know he was released from any obligation to respond, that he was, of course, free to say and do as he pleased. Would it make it any easier for him if I apologized for the invitation? I started to speak, but L closed his eyes. Another warm glance, down at his shoes, and then a little smile. He was so determined to interrupt me. He would not have me humiliate myself. "I'm very sorry," L simply said.

He explained he wished he could get away. He was very sorry he couldn't. He wasn't sure he could. He had very little free time, and hardly any money. He would just have to wait and see.

L said he would certainly be glad to talk with me about that another time.

In the evening we went to the movie together. I knew my feelings. We sat a bit apart, separated by others. I did not want to force him to reject me.

When we met at breakfast the next morning he told me he had brought back a present from New York. "If you like I will give it to you," he said. "You must come to see me whenever you want it."

I was flattered, flustered. I had to turn away from him and close my eyes. The face I showed him when I turned back was not mine.

That same morning I came back later to see him in his room. He made coffee for me. We talked together slowly, softly. We could only just seem to make the surface of our feelings known. We still were afraid of each other. I thought I must tell L about my other friend, but he withdrew into his customary advisory manner. "It is sometimes more pleasant," he explained, "to keep some distance with certain persons at a place like this."

I was in such a rage.

Just as I got up to leave L said, "Wait a minute." He went to his bureau and pulled open a drawer to find my present, a piece of pottery, very ancient, and chipped off in places, without any formal design, or color. It was just bare, bluish grayish glaze on one side and dried blood the color of terra cotta on the other.

It was really nothing. It had once been something. It was very beautiful, rather heavy. The threat you felt when you held it was that it might all crumble into dust.

My pleasure with the gift was so intense it was like a

headache. When I left his room I was trying to keep myself from crying.

She had gone away for the day to visit her son at camp with a friend. When we spoke on the phone she seemed so far out of my life it was like holding on tightly to one end of a snapped thread. She would be back very late. She would be sure to leave me a note. She felt she needed to see me again, that her loneliness required it. I must tell her all about myself now, again. I mustn't hide from her anymore.

I was with L. We had just returned from a swim. My typical response to her excitement was to feel both gay and gloomy. I didn't have anything to tell her. I had nothing to hide, or to boast about. She seemed so very young. That was the measure of our alikeness—a common feeling of immature possibilities, a certain terror, and incompleteness.

I said we must surely speak tomorrow.

The sooner the better, she insisted.

I thought I really wanted to see her—tomorrow.

When?

Since I couldn't be sure I knew, she said she would stay with her friend.

The strangeness of it was not to know if I really cared or not. Putting the phone down, pushing it away from me, it seemed as if all our passion had been excess. But now that the panicky time between was over I felt a softening tenderness for her again. I was very unhappy with myself. For being so vulnerable to her moods.

She was clutching. I knew it. She knew it. I felt she must surely know me by now as I knew her and her needs and loved her for them.

A little later she called back. She said she loved me. She said she already felt she knew me better than anybody else in her life. She had been lying to me before. She really was afraid to be with someone else. Whenever she returned she would try to come to see me. She understood I could not leave to be with her. Her feeling was much the stronger of the two. She said she really needed me.

I was in a public place. I told her that too. When she came back we would be able to speak. I felt her need. I told her I couldn't speak.

But when she came back I was tongue-tied again, shattered, startled by myself, surprised into another passion for her. She seemed to be taunting me again. I had told her nothing. She was always being asked to guess about me. Why? She never knew who I was.

Inside myself I was all bunched up like a dirty sock. I didn't think I wanted her to see me that way. If she would not agree in advance to think she knew me how could I possibly come out for her.

We went up to my room. She said our lovemaking was the best ever. I thought of myself as a failure. I did not need good opinions from her. I felt nothing for her except the desire to make her feel me. It was like wishing to wound her.

But she seemed so young she had not known.

In the morning we went down to breakfast together and sat among the others for the first time. It was hard for

me to look at any other person. I felt her eyes. We were silent. I wanted her to come back upstairs with me. I was
afraid to ask, and even more afraid to make this new demand on myself. The day seemed much too short. I found I
had so many errands to perform.

Later at lunchtime we all went swimming. L was
there. The three of us wanted to be friendly. We could not
speak. I think she told herself she didn't want to know L,
and I could see he was being shy with her. He did not wish
to make himself seem genial. He had other feelings.

When we excused ourselves to walk back to the main
house, I left her, suddenly, without saying a word. I wanted
to be by myself to read. I had done so little reading lately. It
did not matter what I read. I wanted to withdraw, to find
pleasure in the thoughts of another person. I had been keeping company with my feelings for so long I felt lonely, ancient, imperious, bowed, like a nobody again. I thought a
book might bring me back to myself.

But I had lost sight of myself and was too lazy to find
my way back. The words with which I struggled to see myself were only another person's words. For the moment I
was happy with them as words, just words, moments of
sound into which I could sink. I glanced through a number
of books. The words gave me pleasure when I let them. I
found nothing of myself.

Just before supper time L came to me again. He would
say nothing, only smile. He seemed just to want to sit with
me. He asked me to go on reading. He wanted me to understand again that he liked me and was not afraid of me. His

need to be by himself was as strict as mine. I tried to smile, but I felt like a certain joke about myself which I could never bring myself to tell to others.

"I have a feeling," L said, at last, with eyes glistening, "you are not used to much calm . . ."

My nod meant I had to agree.

"You think you want intensity," L said, "and you are afraid of it . . . That's why you are here . . ."

I had no easy answers to make to him. With tears I went away from him, still sitting in my room, to see her.

She was with somebody else, her friend. They were talking so intensely that I felt I was intruding. Very quickly the spell was broken by my presence. I started to go but she insisted I stay on. If I could not stay now she would see me later. But why couldn't we all sit together?

She seemed uncertain about her question. I was also trying to make up my mind. Her friend seemed contemptuous of us. Abruptly he got up and excused himself. He had a phone call to make before dinner. Alone with her I found I had nothing to say to her again. She was staring off into space where her friend had vanished. Abruptly she called out to him: EDDIE, WE MUST ALL BE SURE TO HAVE DINNER TOGETHER.

I really don't know what it feels like to be a liar. Going away from her then I didn't bother to show my feelings, and at dinner would not ask L to join us. He would surely only be made unhappy with the combination.

Later I went back to my books. I would read some more, a travel book about Greece. Perhaps I could imagine myself already being there. A chink had fallen from the solid wall blocking me. That was L's present. I must remember to describe my pleasure in it for him.

Her knock on the door interrupted me. It was past eleven on my watch. She knocked a second time and then came right into my room.

"I'm interrupting you . . ."

"Not really . . ."

"I had to see you . . . to tell you some things . . ."

"What now?"

"I'm not the person I told you I was . . ."

"I already know that."

"I do love you . . ."

"So you tell me . . ."

"Do you think we could still have fun together?"

"I'm afraid that's all I was trying to do," I said, "and you kept wanting something more, something else. You kept telling me all those things about yourself. Now I just don't know. I don't really know myself very well anymore. I'm sorry. You've confused me . . ."

"I'm sorry. I know. I still think I happen to love you . . ."

LET'S NOT TALK ABOUT THAT . . .

She nodded, but when she left I thought I saw her face hardening. I became panicky, for her sake as well as my own. "What's the matter?" I cried out. "What is it?"

"You don't really care . . ."

"That isn't true . . ."

She didn't want to hear me. Her voice was controlling

a shrillness. She complained to me bitterly: "When I told you I didn't want to be with anybody else you wouldn't let me have it that way. You were always saying, how do you know if you haven't ever been? I was just with my friend. We tried. It was very sweet and nice. It was not like being with you . . ."

"I don't happen to care to know that!"

I was very angry with her. She could tell. Did she know why? I was afraid to tell her. She had hurt me and she had hurt her friend too. She had hurt herself. By cheating on all of us. For being that frightened I hated her.

She started to explain, and her voice was choked. There were tears in her eyes. She seemed to want her sacrifice appreciated. I was to be grateful for her melodrama, her wastefulness, her disregard of others. I felt such a strong contempt when I took her in my arms to make love to her.

Afterward she seemed as grave and troubled as L. She had loved the experience and she had not. She wondered about me again. Was I really the person I said I was?

We came down the stairs in the big house to look for company to dispel our gloom. L was in the TV room. Glibly, I asked how he was feeling. Before he could reply, she said she wanted to be excused. She'd come to see me later.

When I was alone with L his face broke down a little and he seemed distraught. He seemed to want to talk, but also to remain isolated. He told me he had just called the City to speak to his friend. His smile commenced uneasily. It clouded over him again. *He had just called his friend in the City. Did I understand?* He would say no more. How could I ever understand? He seemed to be testing me. Could I? Because he knew I saw him so clearly it was very frightening to him.

I went across the room to him and touched his shoulder lightly. I wanted him to know I cared. I was glad to see him. I would try to help.

But he began to drift away from my glance.

I tried to pursue him with words, a look, vaguely. "Was it an upsetting call? How do you really feel?" But it seemed to me that my solicitude was gloating.

L's face was tightening around that smile, but then he seemed to blink himself open again, and softened, like a breath expelled against a cold glass surface. The ancient astute philosophical mask with which he stared at me was not his face, but it would do as a substitute. His voice was musing. He seemed to sparkle a bit in the lamplight.

"You must know what it's like with some people. When they behave just as you'd always known they would it hurts you so. It's as if you were always somehow hoping they would be that way or wouldn't. You'd known them all along . . ."

We walked onto the porch into the night air. The gnats were heavy. They bothered both our faces. L frowned. I was worried about him, afraid to offer feelings of love.

I tried to seem hopeful. "Sometimes," I said, "I think we choose our friends so they will always be that way with us."

L seemed to think I was being critical of him. "You mean so they will disappoint?"

Gravely I nodded back.

He seemed extremely sad, and hurt, almost contemptuous again. He was much too complicated. I wasn't understanding him because I was much too young. All that was in the look he pointed at me.

I said, "Sometimes it helps to share experience . . ."

His reply was acid: "This isn't any self-fulfilling prophecy. It's a fault of character, I think. Some people are just emotionally immature . . ."

He was no longer talking about his friend. I could tell. He was staring very hard at my head, as if I was a gnat he wanted to brush away from his face, as if I was hurting him by seeking to come any closer to him, and his only protection was this distance and contempt.

"I mean you no harm," I said. "I never have. Don't you understand? I have feelings too."

He blinked coldly at me, with heavy-lidded eyes. He was no longer listening to me. He seemed so old and hurt in a place I could never hope to reach because he would never trust me enough to open himself to me that far.

L would never trust anybody.

"Goodnight."

He spoke my name, and smiled at me correctly enough. For a moment he seemed almost young again.

Then he drifted away another time.

HAVE A GOOD TIME

One very soft New England fall, when the air was golden, warm, almost dusty—like a pollen—I fell in love. Odd that it should have happened then. I had known Janna a very long while, had left a wife and child to be with her. We had a relationship which all our friends admired. We had even lived together, a tenderness for Janna which I had never allowed for any other person, but even when we were together I had always felt myself limited by our circumstances. To be so adored—my spirits jagged higher and higher; always I was too busy or too distraught to let that feeling take me.

With Janna I was always just about to fall in love, as if she deserved that much from me, when something or other would distract me: sex, my work, guilt over the family I had left behind, other friendships, our hard-won intimacies, or the need I sometimes felt for a solitude which I had never quite allowed myself to experience in earlier life. But now that I had achieved the means of that solitude, at last, I also found myself loving somebody, as if all that heavy autumnal air surrounding me had closed me off from Janna, carrying her away from me. All those brilliant leafy colors in that faint warm chill of light—they seemed dimmed by our absence from each other, as inevitable, or so I thought, as loss.

Yet I had gone away from her. Why did it feel so much like she was leaving me? Perhaps because I had only found the courage to depart at her urging. For years I had wished to be alone with myself for awhile to begin to write

poetry again. Always I had mocked or squelched the appe-
tite. I was always so petty toward myself. So very small and
grudging and guarded. Had I so very little self-respect?
Then it was a wonder Janna had loved me at all.

In love she was able to see me. She could not allow me
any longer to escape my own poetry. "If you think you
must get away," she told me once, "I don't want you ever
feeling as if you're running away." But I began to resent her
insistence that I permit myself a separate destiny. Was it
only that she cared so much for me? Or did I still lack the
imagination to truly see and know her, thinking she had
grown bored or restless in my company and that she was
driving me from town so that she could be more freely herself with other men.

On the day I was supposed to leave I berated her
sorely: "This isn't really what I need. I don't think I can
make it alone . . ."

"You'll have a good time. I know you will."

"I'll miss you . . ."

"But I'll be here," Janna replied, "you can always
come back . . ."

"Suppose I can't . . ."

"Then don't . . ."

"What about you?"

"I'm not the one who's going away . . ."

"You'll meet somebody else . . ."

"Even if I did he would not be you to me."

Much too fearful for our love, I did not question her
further about what she meant. Or was I afraid to let her

know I cared very much that there could be another person, different from me to her, whom she could still love?

It was one of those final summer days that seem to take forever leaving us with night as I drove north through the gray towns of southern New England, feeling my own shabbiness keenly. I had been making such ill use of myself with Janna lately. Of course, I could always come back. But would I? How? Unless I could come back to Janna almost as I had once known her, I didn't suppose I wanted to trust to the risk.

Yet I had never wanted her to come with me. Not from the start. When she told me she thought of staying in the city until I returned I felt so relieved that she would be the person committing us to that separateness which was in my feelings too. Janna . . . *always the courageous one, always so able to state those feelings we shared.* So now that we had parted and I was alone in this woods, miles from any of my nearest friends, with only the radio and a few small birds and animals for company, I knew suddenly that I had been reconnected to certain feelings for her by this act of disengagement. Funny, I don't think I was ever in love with another person that way in all my life.

Ever so close, you might say, as if that gap, that distance, between us now seemed to be inviting us to come more closely together.

I wrote: "I'm not going to be your problem any more because I'm in love."

I felt the most extraordinary sense of well-being; a calm was about to enter our lives. There were sudden throbbing moments of joy and remembered pleasure. A part of myself had now been mapped out, charted, known. There wasn't any further need to live within the unsettling fear of being unloved or unloving.

Love isn't painful, as some poets still insist; nor is it always altogether sudden, unexpected. It's a slow recognition, and that is why I sometimes think there is no such thing as unrequited love. If it is unrequited then it is probably not love. Our intentions vary. Janna wished to show me how much she cared for me by allowing to me that ecstacy of apartness that draws us always back again, closer, to another human being.

Had this ever happened to me in the past? Then why did I think it could happen now when I still imagined I had proved myself so untrue to our relationship by leaving it flat?

Janna was young. I had already lived half a life. That freedom so implicit to her she wanted me to see in myself. I thought she was even willing to take a chance on an interlude of isolation in the city for herself if I could be myself in poetry, through my writing again; and then—afterward, we might be so much more intimate.

But, having reluctantly come to be alone with myself, I found I had Janna on my mind initially quite a good deal of the time; not my city cares of a wife and child left behind, or cares over the money I lacked, or jobs I would have to find when I returned. I had escaped the social grudge, the hateful face of the world, and even my most intimate fleshly thoughts, in a sense, but found I could not escape caring for

Janna: that she had cared so much for me; that she had shown me how to care by loving me enough to let me go. Now that I was away from her there was a slow crumbling movement inside me; all my defenses were slipping away.

Those first few weeks I moved on sea legs over my own quiet footsteps on the pine forest paths. The queer shifts in time that follow the abandonment of an old routine were made uneasy with hazings of memories. I saw myself constantly on all those occasions we had once shared. All those times I had failed at loving her, those times I had failed to observe the joy of her gift to me . . . More than once, we had had to talk more than was necessary to be together.

Had she recognized the recent edge of deference in our love-making?

Had she always known that I had lacked what she could give of herself so loosely, easily? If we were ever to be together again there were so many ways I wished to be content with her—not simply to make amends—that it seemed as if I was only convincing my temerity all the more that I would never be with Janna again.

"Maybe you can find a better person," I seemed to be saying to her.

It was foolish of me, of course; we cannot shop for those we are to love. We can only be moved by what we allow ourselves to see, and feel, and know. Perhaps it was my very lack that was so appealing to Janna. She saw me, recognized me, and was moved to love me, not because I was worthy or unworthy of her, but because I was myself— a man who is so much more than his own low opinion of himself. Now I knew that Janna could not be so easily fobbed off to another by any process of my imagination unless I wished to return to my own lovelessness. Never to love again. I found I still needed and wanted my try at solitude, but I did not want to be that lonely, ever again.

During those weeks in which we corresponded often it was always, as it were, without speaking. What did I wish to avoid? The rushing sense of our former presences swarmed about me. I wished only to be back with her again, and was afraid now to press any other demands on her except continuing the way I was, as if to go deeper into that solitude might actually show me the way out.

Janna also seemed more shy. Probably she did not wish to make me jealous with adventures that were, or so she said, still so very inconsequential to her, though I think she was aware, too, that we could no longer entrust our feelings to words on a page.

Mostly we wrote about our work. Janna was a painter. I loved her softness at it, that she could find so much color in whiteness, and a light beyond that whiteness so direct it was sometimes blinding to me, and if she was not always moved by my new poems, mostly composed to her, or for her, this was as important for me to know as when she was. I trusted Janna to be honest with me because I needed to feel I could trust, almost as much as I needed her honesty.

Of the splendid New England fall I told Janna what I was seeing mostly through pictures, small, inexpert watercolors dabbed and splashed with hints of my momentary failing intensities; and then, in turn, she gabbled to me about

our friends in New York, the new season, the troubles she
was having finding a part-time job, or an apartment.

I wonder if the truest mood we shared those exquisite
autumn days was not the very silence of our love. Preoccu-
pied with the shape of leaf against leaf, or the slanting of late
sunlights, I wrote little of my experiences, and seemed to be
storing away even less within my being. For the first time
ever I seemed to be alive without any purpose beyond my
own processes. I had stilled a habitual *angst*.

Janna seemed to know me all the better for what I
would not say than I her; and in just a little while, I began to
experience queer elations over color and light that even my
paltry technique with paints could no longer conceal. That
stand of maples burned so russet red across the green shim-
mer of my meadow brought such sudden tears into my eyes
when I surrendered myself to the motion of the brush in my
hand. I was feeling so very much better. I was finding my
childhood again.

Perhaps I grew too young too quickly. At making fires,
picking late berries, walking in woods, or staring up at a
cloud, I soon found within myself the absorption of a child
who has seized rather too wildly upon something—anything—to play with, only to find he is now quite unwilling
to be distracted. This aloneness I now felt was only partly
calming. Sometimes I was just as aware of how fearfully little I needed others.

One day, in afternoon sunshine, I wandered to a pond
in the woods that I had found marked on an old map. A few
frogs sunning themselves on stones and grasses scattered in

splashes as I approached the cool green scum of that water. I leaned far over the grassy bank but could not see the bottom, only the reflected blaze of trees and my dark face among them. I dipped my fingers beneath the cold, almost viscous surface, and then, without caring for the consequences, got up again, undressed, and jumped in.

The numbing was instantaneous. I thrashed my way to the shore, but stayed a moment, numbing myself further, fingers perched against a large slippery rock jutting from the surface.

At last I heaved myself up on grass and lay back against the sun, my body, long in the embrace of that air, seeming so white and glazed and cleansed that I was able to pass dizzily from numbness to a trance of warmth in which I dozed, with a sense of perfect well-being, for some minutes. When I came home I wrote through most of the night without once bothering to reread my words.

The day came when I did not think of Janna at all. There was a slaking off of certain old habits. I no longer bothered to name things to myself. Seeing everything I seemed to be seeing nothing. I wasn't any longer anybody in particular.

Though uneasy, at first, over the meals missed and the letters I wrote and never posted (or never wrote), I gradually grew uneasy with my own unease, as if entranced so much by my inanimateness that I felt, at times, as if I needed another person's supervision.

I think now that I could have been a tree, or an ant, but I was only slipping away from my own self-contempt, and I

felt helpless to resist the process. Did I even want to? The
mood had to be broken if only so that I could know what
exactly I was about. One day I decided to pay a visit to
Janna in the city. I had been away longer than a month and
had not come any closer to another person than a greeting.
Did I simply wish to hold her against my arms again?
Calmly, fully, I wanted to be Janna's lover this one more
brief time, not so much to reinvoke our mutuality, but
selfishly again, utterly selfishly for myself. To experience
myself as I had once been with her, though now, purged of
that old specious self, from this new fine distance of my
closeness to myself, ever so much more clearly, as if to
reckon where I had once been and where I was now going.

I packed early. Before leaving I stopped at the post
office to find mail, a letter from Janna:

You did right to find your own atmosphere.

You had to relax. To know how wonderful you
are to those who love you.

I think I love you more for this than ever. If only
we could see each other more it would mean I did not
have to write such things to you. I have met somebody
I care about very much, and he is here with me now
and I would like to be with him awhile until he has to
go away again.

We'll be seeing each other too. You know that. I
love being with you so very much.

As ever,
Janna

It hasn't happened often in my life that I have been surprised by myself. If I was angry I found it hard to name the feeling. Driving back up through the long winding forest road to my cabin I kept staring into the sun through leaves until my eyes were watering. I entered my large dim room and unpacked, then sat out in the sun another long long while on a little bridge chair, leaning back against the walls of my cabin.

What was I thinking? That it was much too warm for October. I tried to open myself up to a poem: I was a dark forest/invaded by sudden light/that I had come upon/you brooding . . .

I despaired of ever clarifying my syntax. The easy trite facility of words did not help me to experience my mood. Perhaps I was only seeking to woo Janna away from her new friend.

The villainy of feeling only oneself. I had arranged my departure as a test for her love of me. Now that she had failed at that test, which she could not have known she was undergoing, did I have all the excuses I needed to resist caring for her again?

Twilight came as a golden haze burned silvery through those files of forest pine. Something of apples rotting scented the air. I could find no new or special knowledge of myself—only that if I failed to understand Janna's need I should be alone again a very long while.

When I went back into the cabin my nostrils were seized with the dry pepper of last night's ashes. Outside the

air was faintly purple. I thought I should eat. I sat at my
writing table next to the window.

Dear Janna
I was awfully pleased to hear you're having such a
good time with your new friend. I'm having such a
good time, too, though there aren't many people
around. I guess I didn't come here for that.
I'm learning a lot about myself.
When I come back we should have lots to talk about.
   Until then, have fun . . .

   I'm sorry to say we never wrote to each other again.

TIT FOR TAT

Naomi had the biggest boobs in the neighborhood. A fellow gets pretty lonely sometimes. All you want is a feel, a little kindness. Women make demands. Politics? What did I know from that? I was working for my uncle, inoculating beef tongues with a syringe. Water, cereal, sometimes a dose of both we'd give them. I tell you it was a corrupt world.

Wintertime in Brooklyn, and I used to have to spend every afternoon in the back room of my uncle's butcher shop with that damn syringe. "Teach you to want to be pre-med," Uncle Murry said. I was lonely, a newcomer to the neighborhood. Hardly knew any of my schoolmates. All I saw was Naomi and those boobs. So she was a Communist, sue me. I couldn't stand being in that dark stinking back room any longer with those ice cold tongues. Gave me goose pimples. Tongues! What I wanted was warm meat. So I wrote those things in chalk for Naomi all over the schoolyard.

Save Willy McGee!
Southern Trees bear strange fruit!
Don't tread on me!

How the hell should I know what I wrote. I shmeared. That's all! Do me something. I guess I was some kind of activist, and that wasn't any good; it was sort of a bad time to be spreading Red propaganda. Everybody was having the jitters about the Berlin Air Lift. Did I give a shit about what happened to those soap-makers? Naomi kept promising but she wouldn't deliver. She was pretty hysterical with Senator McCarthy this and Senator McCarthy that. Tight-lips I was. I made like Alger Hiss.

Talk. All we used to do was talk. But what pumpkins she had. She used to make me listen to long lectures in the schoolyard about the future. I guess she was indoctrinating me. Granted. But what right did I have to bellyache? She would give me free chalk and a new slogan, and then send me off to work. If I was lucky, Naomi would let me cop a little feel first.

It went on like that for nearly two months—mornings in school, afternoons in the back room of the store with the pickled tongues, and evenings with Naomi, plotting social justice behind the handball court, midwinter too, and my hands were usually like ice. The best I ever got was a finger you know where. Jeez! Here I was supposed to be graduating but with Naomi I couldn't even make the grade. Between me and her it was still kid-stuff. Worse! She was always giving me all kinds of stuff about the Arab refugees in the Gaza Strip! A Jewish girl at that! One day Naomi even had me handing out leaflets in front of the deli. "For peace and friendship among peoples and against the Witch Hunters," she explained, handing me a big bundle. She looked lovely. Under her thin blouse I could see the baby fat. The whole business was straining to pop out below. A vision I tell you, leaning against the bologna counter. I did as I was told, and all I got was a hand job behind the monkey bars. Who could enjoy it? Naomi was rushing off to a meeting somewhere, I felt like a cow being milked.

But, as I say, it was better than being alone in the back room with all those tongues. Besides, I was getting sort of sentimental about Naomi and her friends. They were all nice people in a way. They liked to talk a lot, and maybe they used too many big words. Was that a crime? I even think Naomi liked me a little, since she had nobody else except her aunt Heidi. Only she used to be very businesslike in our dealings. What a creepy time. I was determined to score. She had a brain full of Stalin. Friendly Henry Wallace and the Road Ahead? Crap! Pure unadulterated crap! All I wanted was no more detours. But came Chanukah and Christmas and things got depressing for Naomi. The chimes in the Brooklyn College Library Tower finked out. Bad times had hit Foley Square. The lid was on. Instead of the usual Meadowlands, Shostakovich, and the "Song of the Good Comrade," we were given "Rock of Ages," "Spin the Dradel," and the "First Noel." Naomi said it was thought-control. She wouldn't even buy the nonsectarian bit. She was preaching permanent revolution. But every time I heard about all those people "swept under by powers of darkness that rise," I wondered if it was anything like going down for the count.

I should explain that I had moved to Brooklyn from Miami Beach the previous winter, after my parents were divorced, and I brought with me all the usual Jewish prejudices against prostitutes and jerking-off, but I had some special Southern ones added on for good measure. Guilt was the principal rule in my life. I felt guilty about nearly everything, especially my parents' divorce, although they personally didn't seem to care very much. I also had trouble adjusting to the North.

Miami Beach isn't exactly Dixie, but Negroes did ride in the backs of buses, and you rarely saw them shopping on Lincoln Road. Personally I had nothing against Negroes, but I wasn't very used to them, and I felt guilty about it, especially with Naomi. She and I had our problems. Most of her friends were black. She herself was tallish, rather pale, had long straight honey-colored hair, a nose that turned up, even freckles, but she wore a darkish pancake make-up, liked to keep her face dirty, and really dug spades. I used to get very jealous behind the handball court hearing her tell how the previous summer at Shaker Village Camp she had "given herself for the first time" to a "beautiful boy" who, upon further questioning, turned out to be black and a homo to boot.

"If you can do it with one of them you can do it with me," I used to shout.

"Bigot! Bilbo!" Naomi would say. "Go to hell!"

Who me? Did I need that kind pud-pulling? Never. Naomi really got me where I lived. Before I could touch her again she made me swear that I didn't have anything against Negroes personally, and that I wanted to work for their betterment. I swore. There's no law against swearing. But I still couldn't see why she was being so particular in my case if she was so quick to admit that she was no longer cherry and if, in fact, her initial marauder had been *schwartze*.

"What have I got—spots?" I would howl. "What did he have that I don't?"

"Stupid," Naomi said. "Can't you see? He needed me!"

"Well, what the hell do you think I need?"

"That's the trouble with you," Naomi said. "All you can think about is yourself. Now get your hand away or I'll call the supervisor."

She gave me a knee in the groin, and when I doubled over, handed me a card saying HARRY TRUMAN IS A MURDERER. Passion cramps and all, I went off to chalk up the grandstands in the Brooklyn College football field with Naomi's message.

What a winter that was! When the snow began to melt and the birds came back I wanted to run naked through the streets. Anything to get off my rocks. That was the winter of the Slochower affair and, because of Naomi, I flunked trigonometry and would have to make it up in summer school to graduate. Also, I was tossed out of the Inter-Denominational Chorus and the Inter-Racial Orchestra for nonattendance. To make matters even worse, Uncle Murry promoted me. Itchy Brindberg would be doing the tongue inoculations from now on, and I would be allowed to work behind the counter, serving customers in my bloody apron.

Uncle Murry taught me how to keep my thumb on the scale, how to cut a rib chop "lean," how to weigh the bones in a filet, where to slit open a capon, how to sell fowl for spring chicken, the works, the whole bloody business. And I was now getting fifty-five dollars a week part-time, not including what I cribbed from the register, and feeling corrupt as hell. I even began to believe some of Naomi's slogans. Like "Solidarity forever!" When you got your hand in the meat grinder and you're pushing through gristle, bone, fingernails and wrapping twine, at ninety-five cents a pound, all that stuff can really get to you.

But Naomi and me, we rarely saw each other anymore. Most of the time I was just too fagged out from lugging around those bloody sides of beef. Also, Uncle Murry frowned on Naomi's coming into the store. "Now that you're in business," he would say, "stay away from the Communists."

Murry claimed he didn't like Naomi passing out leaflets in his place. He also resented my giving her the finger in the deep freeze. I couldn't say I blamed him. He had a very high-class clientele, *kosher boser*. Real grade-A shit. Besides, the freezer had glass windows in the doors and Naomi liked to groan and holler a lot when she was with a boy. She also had the annoying habit of buttonholing the ladies as they came through the front door with old newspaper pictures of Mrs. Roosevelt shaking hands with Paul Robeson.

A regular lost cause. What the hell was happening to me anyway? I didn't want to be a butcher the rest of my life but I sure as hell liked those fifty clams a week, and I was scared as hell of cutting open even frogs, much less live things. As Uncle Murry used to say, decapitating a young chicken with one stroke of his ever-sharp cleaver, "Here you got no place to go but . . . DOWN."

"Teach you something about surgery," he would say. Or he would argue: "Who doesn't like to eat meat?"

"Them Communists maybe," Murry would explain, "Is the same as with them with Vegetarians. Dollars to donuts. Don't you worry about them," Murry went on. "It ain't them what makes my top-grade calf's liver move. Dollars to donuts it ain't."

"Boy," he would say, "could I have been a surgeon or a sturgeon. Take your pick."

Uncle Murry went to Florida every spring after the rates went down, so that year I played hookey from school and was left in charge of the shop for two weeks. I did *some* business. Everything went on special. All the *yentahs* pinched me and called me cutey-pie. I let them all think they were getting something for nothing. While Itchy pumped away at his tongues in the back room, I chopped horsemeat, chicken necks, *puppicks*, everything except the cat, and the women bought because I played up to them. God knows how many feels I must have copped across that bloody counter, but they all seemed to have breasts made out of chicken flesh.

It just wasn't the same as with Naomi. These were pushovers. I grew a moustache to hide my harelip. The ladies made goggle eyes, hoping for the best cuts. All I wanted was my usual piece of Naomi.

You want to know something? I actually felt nostalgic for the good old days behind the handball courts, and I missed all those goddamned causes too. The Rosenbergs were hot just then. And we had customers by the same name. They even looked alike: fat with big eyeglasses and a Persian lamb coat. Was I to believe in spy stories? Up yours, I said. When I met Naomi coming from the night depository she swore to me it was a frame-up but all she was willing to give me was bare titty and a slap in the face unless, of course, I wanted to go up to Peekskill that weekend for a demonstration.

That weekend it rained cats and dogs. Peekskill was out of the question. My uncle being the only kosher butcher in Flatbush who kept open on Saturdays, I closed the store early when I saw there was no business. I took thirty dollars with me from the till because I planned to take in a movie and then meet Itchy for dinner at the Chink's. Maybe, later on, we would drift down to Avenue M for some beers. Hell. I wanted to be the big sport that night.

Crossing King's Highway I had on my leather jacket and my seabee hat. I was carrying three pounds of rib steak inside a copy of the *Compass* when who should come along? You guessed it—Naomi Tarnapole.

"You see that rain," she was saying, pointing up to the neon-tinted murky heavens above the marquee of the Kingsway Theatre. "That's what they call fall-out. Radioactive death. Every drop contains an atomic particle, and those particles are enough to kill a horse. Remember Nagasaki? That's what your great America has done. It's raining atom bombs, shmuck. Sign this."

On closer examination I could tell that Naomi hadn't just happened to be out in the rain. She had planted herself dead center in the middle of the blast area. Speaking of shmucks, she had an ordinary clipboard in her hand with a sheet of mimeo paper tucked under it, covered again by a plain white sheet of oil cloth. A number of childish signatures were scrawled across the paper. Naomi was shivering. She had one of those ball-point pens that write under water. "Sign," she urged, handing me the pen.

I would have needed such a pen. The rain was coming down like in my uncle Murry's stall shower. Naomi was drenched, but she sure looked beautiful with all that rainwater dripping and dribbling down her face. I saw her staring at my newspaper. It too was drenched through so that the blood was showing.

"What you got in there?" she asked.

I said: "Thought you were only interested in dark meat."

Whamo! She slammed me across the *punim*.

"Look," I said, startled, "what the hell are you giving me now?"

"Do you want to die?" she screamed. "Do you want to die?"

I said, "Aw shut up and come with me."

I took Naomi by the arm and pulled her with me into the Dubrow's Cafeteria. Then I set our stuff down on a table and helped her pull off her wet things. She was soaked through. I pushed the napkin holder toward her, forcing her to sit down. "Wipe your hair with some of these," I explained. "I'll get coffee."

When I came back off the line with the two steaming cups of coffee on my tray, Naomi was sitting up in her chair, sort of prim, her clipboard under one arm, the damp bosoms in their see-through jersey sort of resting against the edge of the formica table top. She smiled. "I guess I was being a little silly out there."

"Forget it," I told her.

We slurped coffee together. "You really have the potential to be a good person," Naomi said, "and . . . maybe there is hope."

"Thanks," I told her, pushing my chair closer so that my arm could go around her waist.

"Not here!"

Naomi snarled at me between her teeth. I took my hand away again, already conscious of a pulse below my belt. "Jeez!" I said.

"What is wrong with you now?" she asked.

"Naomi," I said, "will you have a heart? You know what's wrong. It's been going on like this with us for four months. What am I supposed to be—Superman? I'll bust my jock over you someday."

"Must you?" she said. "Please, please."

Naomi meant it. I could see she wasn't kidding. She was crying. Real tears too. Not like when they sent up William Remington. Why, she was out of her mind. Her shoulders were trembling. Her face was pale. She seemed like she was going to vomit, and she was spilling coffee in her saucer.

"Naomi," I blurted. "What have I done now? Just what is it?"

"You make me want to throw up, you're so greedy," she said. She wouldn't even look me straight in the eye. Honest. I felt pretty bad. Other people were staring at us.

Every once in awhile we heard the ticket bell at the front entrance going *bong bong, bong bong bong.* Naomi sobbed all the louder. Behind her head mushroom clouds rose from the steam counter. A little boy at the next table had wet his pants.

What a place for sentimentality. Naomi just wouldn't respond to me any longer, though I used every bit I had ever tried: the draft bit, the mulatto bit, the anti-Semite bit, yes, even the war-orphan bit. Naomi just gave me that paranoid, persecuted look while her eyes continued to run like faucets.

Finally I decided to attack from the left. "Honestly, Butch," I said, calling her by her cover name, "must we have all this bourgeois sentimentality?"

Cockeymun! Naomi gagged on her tears but was silent.

"Butch," I continued, "this is hardly the way to act in front of the enemy. Think of Judy Coplan," I added.

"Drop dead," Naomi shot back.

"You too," I replied, just as quickly, but I had lost her again.

"O you . . . you . . ."

She was beating her fists against my chest.

I hastily said, "Well then think of Rosey Luxemburg."

"You big bastard!"

I caught Naomi's hands just in time and pulled her to me. She fell against my chest, a ton of shit, sobbing again. "I been all day," she said, "all day . . . and what have I got? Forty-nine signatures, mostly grade school kids too. If I had fifty I could get to the World Youth Congress in Vienna. What do you think of that? I'd be out of this goddamn neighborhood at last. Vienna. Stockholm. That's something to work for, isn't it?"

I was slipping my hand under her jersey.

"Well, isn't it, Ira? It's no worse than collecting Green Stamps."

"Sure it isn't baby," I said. "Sure."

I kissed away her tears, starting up her skirt with my other hand. Tight-lips again.

"Think of it," she was saying, "a whole summer in Vienna. A visit to East Berlin. The Berliner Ensemble, Chinese opera, sports. Maybe the rain really *is* contaminated. You know any different? Then how the hell should I know? And why did all those old Jewish women have to call me a traitor. *'Curva,'* they kept screaming at me. *'Curva!'* "

"Well that don't necessarily mean you're a traitor," I put in.

Naomi calmed down a bit. She was breathing far more regularly, with a little flutter of passion added on.

"Besides," I told her, "even if the rain isn't full of that stuff maybe it ought to be. Puts lead in the pencil."

Right in Dubrow's I said it.

"After all," I explained, "have you ever taken a deep breath on a rainy day? Stinks! It's from all that filled-in land."

I don't think Naomi was listening to me. I heard her say, "I'm not afraid of Mr. Hoover and his goons."

I was thinking that my mother was in the mountains and that my house was empty.

"I said I'm not afraid of McCarthy or anybody," she whispered fiercely.

"Do you think I am?" I shot right back at her.

A shadow was hovering over our table. "You kids gonna sit here all day over one stinking cup of coffee?"

It was the manager, a fat little man who looked like Morton Sobel.

"Don't worry," I said. "We're leaving in a minute. We just had a little accident. We'll be going now. Don't worry."

I let go of Naomi. We sat up together. In the middle of the table was a puddle of blood from my package of rib steak. The man came with a rag to wipe it clean.

An old woman in Red Cross shoes was saying, "Don't you kids know any better?"

Naomi wiped her eyes with her sleeve: "Class enemy!"

How do I know what I might have said to shut her up then? All I know is Naomi suddenly had her hand in my lap and she was telling me, "You'll sign? You mean it? Don't do it for my sake. Don't do it now if you're afraid. You can get into a lot of trouble, you know. This is a police state."

A regular Japanese massage I was getting, and I had the nerve to ask her, "You ain't jail bait are you?"

As if I knew which side was up.

When Naomi drew away a second, I added: "Come on. We'll have rib steaks and wine and I'll take you to the movies afterwards. The Vogue has *My Son John.* Come on

Naomi, what do you say. Maybe you'd like to go with me to the Chink's?"

"Chinese," she corrected me.

"OK, Chinese," I said, *"mainland Chinese."*

"OK," she brightened.

"OK with me too," I said.

There were tears in her eyes. I put her hand back where it belonged. "Only you gotta go all the way," I warned.

"We're in this together," she replied.

"You betcha."

Slowly Naomi wet her lips with her tongue. The ticket bell was playing the "International." Maybe she was thinking how husbands and wives can't testify against each other. I got more than I bargained for: a roll in the hay, an apartment in Forest Hills, a note on a new car, a baby, a bald spot, and the complete works of Plekhanov, annotated.

Score one for Peace and Friendship among Peoples!

TIMMY

Mrs. Golden's children rarely visited her. She didn't mind, although she told them that she did. Edgar, her husband, was like the children; he was always busy with one thing or another, and that Mrs. Golden didn't care for any of his activities wasn't necessarily his fault. Edgar was a fine provider, an energetic, active sort of man who had gotten quite far rather early in life and thought he should still be going somewhere. The only trouble was his wife hadn't cared to make the trip with him. She had liked it much better in her comfortable home. Bitterly, once, Mrs. Golden had accused Edgar of inspiring the children's neglect for her, but even as she spoke she saw this wasn't so. She knew her husband would have liked the kids to spend more time with their mother if only to relieve him of some of the burden.

Not that you could honestly call Lilly Golden a ball-and-chain; she was far too meek, long-suffering, devoted, and was considered by most strangers to be a good wife. Although she and her husband rarely saw each other (except at breakfast), or spent time with each other (except on those combination business-trip vacations which Edgar liked to take), they knew deeply that their marriage was inextricable in the same way that some dreams make one aware that one is dreaming. If Lilly happened to be awake at night when Edgar would come home from one of his trade banquets or dinner meetings, she would register the proper notes of protest and solicitude at being awakened while always making sure to ask him questions about his day. Drowsy, bored, yet somehow strengthened by her husband's return, Lilly would lie back and listen to Edgar thump about in the darkness while he undressed, proud that she had sustained the loneliness once again. Shuddering when the covers were rolled back, or when Edgar brushed against her with a gross caress, she had schooled herself never to move away. Pretending sleep, she would wait until he had dozed off, and then she would get up, would walk out into the parlor, and stare blankly at the evening paper for an hour or so.

During the day Lilly found that being alone was an exhausting chore. Then she tried hard to be "self-sufficient" in response to Edgar's constant declarations that he was not going to live forever, but as she was not a club woman and did not like to window shop in Manhattan or to go to museums or matinees, the hours dragged. Her three sons, their wives, and the grandchildren might have kept her company, but the daughters-in-law frightened Lilly; the sons were now businessmen themselves; and she knew enough not to want to interfere in the raising of their children. Consequently, her main companion had to be Timmy.

Timmy was about the same age as her mistress and she had been with the Goldens as a day worker ever since the children were infants. The two women got along well. Boisterously, each entertained the other without ever being mean or condescending; with Timmy in the house, Lilly did not need to feel so shut in. From 9 A.M. to 5 P.M. on Mondays, Wednesdays, and Fridays, the two women carried on a running kaffee klatsch and pajama party. At times they giggled together like schoolgirls; at other times Timmy called her mistress "ma'am" and "honey" and never Lilly, but that was merely a convention; they talked to one another like old friends.

Timmy was a tall, heavy-set colored woman who had once been slim and pretty. She had a brazen stare and the skin along her arms and shoulders had a smooth, deep brown luster. Only her high cheekbones and her long delicate eyelashes gave an indication of her former voluptuousness. Otherwise, in her tattered stocking-cap, with her sleeves rolled up above her crinkled elbows, she gave off a perfume of starch and bleaching fluid and affected a plodding, goonish sloppiness in comparison with which Lilly Golden looked withered, skimpy, almost unformed—a frail, not quite blonde woman with narrow hips and shoulders, whose large blue, staring eyes seemed so much brighter than her habitually drab, printed bathrobes. Placed alongside Timmy, Lilly could not help but look meager indeed.

Yet she would spend hours in the kitchen with the colored woman, gossiping, or smoking cigarettes, or just watching those big soft shoulders and strong arms plod through the ironing. "How's your sister these days?" Lilly might ask. ". . . You know the one I mean . . . the one who needs insulin . . . don't you remember? I gave you the money . . ."

"Oh, that one," Timmy would say with a good-natured smile, "that one that has the diabetes," signifying that she had been caught in an earlier lie or an exaggeration. Hurriedly then, as she creaked back and forth against the ironing board, Timmy would find a way to change the subject, or she would begin a long dissertation on the family's squalid condition in far-away Pine Ridge, Georgia. She would squeal, "That reminds me," and then would throw Lilly completely off the scent by quickly narrating one harrowing New York adventure, followed by a second one, in the process of which the names of dozens of exotic gin mills, movie theaters, barbecues, and hotels might be summoned up as evidence. Tying her bathrobe tightly about her waist, Lilly would sit cross-legged on the kitchen stool, a shrewd inquisitor. She could always tell when Timmy was lying, but she never cared to catch her up and make her stammer; she preferred to hide her secret glee behind the terry-cloth lapels of her robe.

Because Timmy had never married, to Lilly's knowledge, the first question every Monday would invariably be: "How was your weekend? How did the boys treat you?"

Then Timmy's thick, tinted lips would break into a rare frown. "Missus Goldenhoney," she would say, wiping a hand along her bandana, "sometimes I think them men creatures oughtn't to be allowed to carry on the way they do."

What followed then would be a salty discourse concocted half of Bessie Smith and half of Mary Worth. Timmy's escapades with the men of Harlem or Bedford-Stuyvesant had not ceased at the menopause. They always seemed to begin with her stepping out with one man, losing track of him, then running into a second, an even older friend. But, despite the inept plotting, the years had taught Timmy to color such improbable yarns to Lilly's satisfaction with numerous strandlike asides and great quantities of a dark rhetoric of the streets that permitted her to invent infinite epithets with which to allude to the act of love, or to such actions as dancing, boozing, or even singing in a church choir. All these experiences breathed life when Timmy told them, and the result was that Mrs. Golden might frown, or sigh, or make little clucking noises of disapproval with her tongue, but she would find herself muttering, "Ah yes," and, "Go ahead," and "Then what happened?"

Even over lunch, the colored maid's lusty monologue might continue. If Timmy was too busy with her housework, Mrs. Golden would prepare the sandwiches and brew tea. Then they would sit down opposite each other. Later, if it was a nice day, Mrs. Golden might get dressed to do her shopping. Otherwise, she would order by telephone and they would spend the afternoon in more talk, with Lilly following Timmy about the house to issue the kinds of instructions which after twenty years were no longer necessary.

Usually, then, the two women would talk in a confidential way about the Golden family. In the master bedroom, Mrs. G would pitch in with the moving and lifting of heavy objects as she related what a busy man her husband was; one at a time, through her sons' deserted lairs, she would discuss what eventually should be done with the various pieces of sporting equipment, books, records, and souvenirs that still lay around on the tops of night tables and bureaus, catching dust; or she would show the maid the newest snapshots of her grandchildren, or tell her dry, uninteresting

stories of their latest antics. In the face of all this, Timmy
played her role convincingly; she was polite without ceasing
for a minute to attend to her chores. She made no secret of
the fact that she didn't like any of the other Goldens.
"Them," she called the children, and Lilly no longer
winced when she heard the word. She was much too pleased
that she could have this intimacy with Timmy and she
never felt that she was permitting the girl liberties. When
Edgar asked if she had paid "the schwartsa," she did not re-
buke him, for she knew the name was important to him for
his image of himself, but she almost never used such a word
herself, and if she did she crossed her fingers. The fact was
that when her maid had left the house Lilly Golden thought
only about her next visit.

That is why, when Edgar died suddenly in his sleep of
a heart attack, Timmy was the first person she wanted to
come and be with her.

The children lined up solidly against that idea. On the
morning of the funeral, when the maid was out of earshot in
the kitchen, they argued that Lilly could afford a real companion, a college girl or another widowed lady like herself,
not just a colored maid. They also suggested that Mrs.
Golden sell the house and move into an apartment nearer
the city. When Lilly raised her voice in protest, her eldest
son puffed out his cheeks just like Edgar, and declared:
"Mother, please. We know you're still upset."

It rained for the funeral, and the cold, dreary affair
went off according to a precise timetable. There were the
usual number of staged and unstaged outbursts; there was

even a moment of genuine pathos for Lilly when the coffin was lowered into the grave and she found that she could not release the pocket of dirt that had been thrust into her hands. Afterward, she and the children returned to the old house for a cold luncheon prepared by Timmy, but Lilly retired as soon thereafter as possible, and when, early the next morning, the children returned for a visit along with two of Edgar's brothers, the assistant rabbi, and the family lawyer, Lilly greeted them by announcing her plans with dry eyes.

She would keep the big house and ask Timmy to sleep in. She did not want to go away on a trip; she did not think it would be fair to live in White Plains with her eldest son; she did not want her sister in Minneapolis to come and stay with her awhile. "We never got along when Edgar was alive. Why should we now?" Lilly asked. "Besides," she added, "Flora has no sense of humor and Timmy does." She preferred Timmy, or to be left alone, if need be, for she wanted time to think. Patiently, Lilly explained that just so long as she had someone to do the heavy cleaning and cook for her occasional guests, she would be happy, but her second son, Robert, exclaimed: "Honestly, Mamma, it sounds so impractical."

Lilly didn't deny that it was. "That's the way I want it . . . and I can afford it," she simply said.

"Besides," she smiled vaguely again, as if her colorless smile and her colorless voice were conspiring together, "I won't be lonely. There's TV and the telephone and a great big world outside."

"But Mother . . ."

Lily held up her hand to demand silence. "If all else fails, I'll have my memories," she said.

This sentiment took everybody by surprise. The three sons thought: "She means memories of us." The daughters-in-law smiled guiltily together. "Jesus," went the astonished lawyer, and even Edgar's brothers mused: "Memories of him. The old girl liked him after all. God help her."

Then, because none of the sons had wanted Lilly to move in with them in the first place, one by one they relented and it was agreed that she was to do as she pleased, as long as the situation was manageable, if she would release some of the money from the estate to compensate the younger Goldens for the valuable property on which the house stood.

Wearily, Lilly agreed. It was small blackmail for her freedom, she thought, as she signed all the necessary papers, kissed her children, and made them promise to visit her often with the little ones. Then the lawyer had to go and Edgar's brothers sat around coughing, whispering, and glancing at condolence cards, before they, too, departed.

On the very next morning, Timmy came to work late as usual, but Mrs. Golden didn't make her intentions known to the girl on that day or the next, for she was still too busy receiving visitors, and when the last of these had departed, she preferred to remain alone in her room. It was not that Lilly felt timid. On the contrary, she felt sure that Timmy would be more comfortable in that large suite of rooms in her attic than in some Harlem tenement, and she had promised herself not to impose any restrictions on the maid. If she didn't make the invitation right away, it was because she wanted to endure her isolation for just a little while longer; for the moment, it gave her a kind of joy.

Ever since that morning when she had opened her eyes to find Edgar dead alongside her, Lilly had hardly a moment to make her peace with that part of her life that began and ended with Edgar. To be finally alone was like waking from a bad dream to be assured by somebody you wanted to trust that the dream had been a fact and now the real dream was to start; and when she looked down into Edgar's rude, cold eyes for the last time, Lilly wondered if it weren't all hallucination. How else had she ever been tamed by such a man? Death had twisted Edgar's lips and blanched his cheeks, turning his expression sullen and pathetic. How then had he managed to frighten her so in their former life together? When she was alone she pondered this question as she meandered about the big house in her peignoir, going from room to room, throwing out letters, magazines, and papers without discrimination, save for the fact that she touched everything that had once been Edgar's with a faintly pleasurable sense of dread.

For nearly two weeks she lived that way. Timmy was given a vacation with pay; for a few days the phone was lifted off its cradle; and she told her family not to worry and not to try and see her for awhile. Getting up when she pleased and going to sleep when she pleased, Lilly Golden drew the shades about her, threw away the stacks of black-edged cards without acknowledging them or the wreaths and flowers from her late husband's Gentile friends, and lived for the most part on coffee and on the baskets of fruits and sweets that kept arriving. She wandered through the house, her eyes glancing from the television set to the sliver of daylight beneath the drawn shades, or to the ancient sepia photos of her husband and the babies that were on the mantel, and while she made preparations for her new mode of life, she was not stirred to thoughts of Timmy. But on the Monday of the third week after Edgar's death, the maid returned.

It was a warm, springish day in late March when Lilly woke up quite late in the morning from a dream about New Orleans, where she had spent her honeymoon, to find that the shades had been raised and that the sun was streaming across her face brightly. At first, she was alarmed by all the sunshine and the ringing stillness to the air, until she detected Timmy's familiar whistle coming from downstairs in the kitchen. Then she looked up and noticed that the television was still lit from the night before with tiny incandescent specks, although it made no noise now save for a low, steady, shushing sound. Lilly jumped out of bed. She rushed to the machine and flicked the switch. Slipping into her robe, she hurried out of the room and down the hall to wash her face and comb her hair in the bathroom. Presently, she was hurrying again toward the stairway when she stopped herself short, cinched the belt on her robe once more, and began to walk downstairs slowly into the kitchen.

The first thing she saw was Timmy's broad bent back.

"Good morning," she called to the girl, who had already set up her ironing board and was going over the last of Edgar's shirts.

Between puffs of steam, Timmy lifted her head gracefully. "I got your juice ready," she announced, without yet looking around.

Lilly's glance went to the counter near the sink, where Timmy had placed a setting for breakfast. There was light toast in the salver and the percolator stood on the stove, warmed by a smudge of blue flame. On the ironing board, alongside Timmy's elbow, a cold cup of coffee stood.

"Why, that's very sweet of you," Lilly said, trying still to get the girl to turn around. She went toward the counter.

"Maybe you should give the juice a stirring," Timmy suggested.

"Yes, I will . . . of course," murmured Lilly, glancing sideways as she walked past and noticing Timmy's bright green pinafore and the new pink bandana that held her straight hair in place against her head. At the counter she spun around and met the girl full face. She had expected a smile but was greeted with a stare and a slow look of irony around the corners of the mouth. "You look well," Lilly said.

Timmy nodded: "Uh huh."

"Very well indeed," Lilly added. As she downed her juice with a quick toss of the head, she heard the iron sizzle against the shirt front. Then Mrs. Golden walked to the stove and poured herself some coffee. Lighting a cigarette, she sat down on the kitchen stool, simultaneously kicking her bright gingham slippers off her feet and curling her white toes around the chrome stool support, to watch Timmy glide over the shirt front and to sip her coffee.

"Well?" she asked.

And again: "Well?"

But the maid was reluctant to start a conversation, so Lilly finally had to add: "Well, how was your vacation?"

Timmy pretended to frown. "Trouble," she mumbled, "nothing but trouble, expense, and aggravation."

Lilly's heart began to pound. Then, aloud, she heard Timmy add: "Didn't even get to Pine Ridge. Didn't get nowhere. Stayed home most of the time with Bill and watched teevee. Well, you know," she explained rather archly, as if an explanation was in order, ". . . Bill . . . he's my new fella . . . he don't like to go nowheres . . ."

"Oh?"

Timmy's body heaved. She dipped the ends of her fingers under the dripping sink and sprinkled the area around the blue ESG monogram on Mr. Golden's shirt. Tiny currents of steam shot out when she placed the hot iron over the monogram. "God damn Bill," she mumbled grouchily.

"Men are like that sometimes," Lilly said, trying to console her.

"Oh, but I didn't mean," Timmy started to say, before succumbing to a giggle. Then she smirked: "You said it, sister. You're lucky to be done with all that. Maybe Jewish men are different . . ."

"No." Lilly shook her head. Then she decided to be

bold. "I didn't know you had a new man," she said. "Tell me about him. What's his full name? What is he like? What does he do?"

The smile faded from Timmy's lips. "Name's Bill," she replied, folding Edgar's shirt and reaching down into her wicker basket for another damp white bundle. "Bill don't do nothing much," she added with a grunt.

"Oh, Timmy. I'm sorry," said Lilly again. The expression had been formed without her choosing it. She had expected more from Timmy—a story, a ribald explanation of Bill's do-nothing attitude—but that was no reason for her to be sorry, and when the maid remained silent as she wrung out the shirt between her pudgy, dark pink hands, she wished she could recall the phrase. "He don't do nothing . . . that one," she heard Timmy say, almost belligerently, bending low over the plane of the board now so that her ample bosoms were pendant behind the pinafore, and when she saw her reach for the hot iron again, Lilly suddenly blurted: "Timmy . . ."

The maid looked up.

". . . I don't know whether it's necessary for you to do Mr. Golden's shirts with such care now," Lilly said.

Timmy's smooth forehead was dense with perspiration and her hand was clutching the iron. "No, ma'am?" she asked, incredulously.

"No," Lilly announced, gaining courage. "As a matter of fact, there's a lot of Mr. Golden's stuff lying around that we ought to organize and throw away. I tried to do some things when you were gone, but I didn't know where to begin or what to do with certain items. There's all his suits, for instance. Some are like new. My husband was quite a dandy, you know. Maybe your Bill can use them?"

"*No, ma'am. Not Bill,*" the maid spoke loudly and sternly. She stared hard at Lilly as if delivering a prepared lecture. "Bill wouldn't like no hand-me-downs . . ."

Lilly's throat went dry: "I see . . ."

Turning away, she tried to close her eyes, to shut the incident from her thoughts, to dissociate herself from this second blunder. She realized she might have offended her old friend by offering a dead man's clothes to her new lover. Negroes, she knew, were apt to be superstitious. But she had meant no offense. She swore she hadn't. She had only thought that Bill might want to make use of such nice clothes. Walking barefoot to the stove to pour herself a second cup of coffee, Lilly could feel Timmy's eyes upon the back of her neck, and she was aware of a strong, cheap perfume. "Ma'am?" she heard. Spinning around so that she spilled some of the coffee into the saucer, Lilly saw the maid staring down at the wilted monogram on the damp white shirt.

She whispered. "Yes?"

"Ma'am," Timmy's lips moved again.

"Yes," she replied.

"Maybe you don't understand what I meant . . ."

"Oh, never mind," Lilly interrupted.

"But Mrs. Goldenhoney . . ."

"Timmy, I think I understand and I certainly didn't mean to offend your Bill; however, I do think we ought to try and dispose of these things, come what may."

She waited patiently for the colored woman to agree with her, but when not another word was said, Lilly lit a fresh cigarette from the still-smoldering butt end and began to speak again in a hoarse, croaking voice. "Timmy," she asked then, "along these lines . . . what would you say . . . how would you like a full-time job?"

Timmy gave no sign that she had understood. She brushed the sweat off her forehead and again started to lift the iron.

"Didn't you hear what I asked you?" Lilly's throat began to hurt. "Do you understand what I mean?"

The maid breathed heavily. "I heard you and I understan' and I was thinkin' about it . . ."

"Well . . . what do you think?"

"Well, now, Mrs. Goldenhoney, I think that's darn nice of you, but, ma'am"—she smiled—"you see, I don't know's if Bill would like that idea . . ."

"But he can sleep in with you. What is there not to like about it?"

"Oh . . . you know." The maid turned shy.

Lilly could no longer contain her curiosity. More than ever before, she felt that she did not know and that Timmy was not trying to understand what she had offered her. "Do you always do what this Bill likes you to do?" she asked sharply. Then: "Why him and not the others?"

Timmy mimicked shock. Her mouth fell open. "Be-

cause Bill . . . he ain't like any of the others," she said, and
when Lilly didn't let on that she had understood, Timmy
added: "I mean he's different . . . treats me good. Them
others . . . they don't give a good goddamn for old Timmy
. . . all except Bill. . . . He's serious with me. Now do you
understan'?"

She paused to see if her message had been understood
before adding, with another curious heave of her shoulders:
"Matter of fact . . . Bill, he say he don' want me to work
here at all no more. He say I could do much better in a factory. But I keeps telling him about you and how you needed
me now that the Mister is passed away and he say okay . . .
okay, maybe you should stay on awhile, Timmy, until she is
straightened out with the estate and can move in with her
folks . . ."

The maid's voice trailed off as she saw Mrs. Golden
clap her hands over her burning ears. Then it rose again for
a moment, but Lilly clearly was no longer listening. The
dullest of headaches was coming on her and she had already
begun to reply in an uncanny echo of a voice: "That's very
understanding of Bill. Thank you, Timmy. Bill is very understanding and you are being too kind . . . but . . . I
hadn't planned to move in with my *folks* ever . . ."

Timmy interrupted: "Mrs. Golden, you oughtn't to
talk that way . . ."

"Why not?" Lilly cried. *"Don't you understand that I
don't like them any better than you do?"*

The maid did not answer. She merely shook her head
as a further warning to Lilly before turning away to resume

her ironing. And Lilly, wanting to beg her now to stop, became strident: "*Why are you treating me like this?* You're lying again, aren't you? You . . ."

But in the middle of that last sentence, a sudden surge of humiliation went through her. The extent of her own impudence became unbearable as she perceived that Timmy would never have considered such an arrangement even if there had been no Bill. Then Lilly felt terribly meager and embarrassed in the presence of the stout, complacent colored woman. She pushed aside her stool and walked to the doorway. But spite got the better of her once again. Turning, she announced: "I am going upstairs to dress. Then I am going shopping. When you get a chance I want you to clean out Mr. Golden's closet. Keep anything you think Bill will like. I'm sure he can't be *that* particular."

"Uh huh."

That special grunting sound of the maid's pierced Lilly's being, draining the spite from her so that—for a moment—she stared at the stolid figure bent low over the ironing board with a quiet tenderness, but when she tried to imagine Timmy once more as she had in her fantasies, her eyes filled with tears and she had to flee upstairs.

Twenty minutes later a hot bath had revived her sufficiently to allow her to dress and stand fully clothed for the street on the top landing. As she went down the stairs, Lilly heard Timmy vacuuming and humming to herself in the living room. She said nothing to the maid as she rushed out onto the front steps, but when she returned from the super-

market and the bank an hour and a half later, still wide-eyed
from the unaccustomed glare of day, Timmy had fled. The
old house was deserted once more. The shutters banged; the
floors rang with her footsteps; and there was not even a note
left behind, although Timmy had not taken any of her uniforms and had carefully placed Edgar's shirts on the bed
above her pillow.

That evening Mrs. Golden could not sleep. As she lay
in the darkness of her room with her eyes open she imagined as if in a dream that Timmy had been caught in a tenement fire and was dying of burns. Rushing to the hospital
by taxi, she knew that she would offer to forgive the maid,
but when she was ushered into the dingy, tiled hospital
room she saw Edgar's naked white body lying on the bed.

She cried out.

Early the next morning a man called on the telephone.

Timmy was taking a job in a factory, he said. She was
not going to do housework anymore. Whatever was still
owed, Mrs. Golden could send care of Bill Dawson at Post
Office Box E 120, Bronx 11, N.Y.

"Did you write that number down?" the man asked.

Sprawled across her bed, Lilly Golden swallowed pain-
fully as she assured the man that she had copied the address.

"Timmy says it comes to twenty-nine dollars and sev-
enty-five cents for three days plus carfare and for you to
send a money order, not a check," the man said then.

"All right," went Lilly, before realizing that she had
something more to say, a message to give. She added: "I

hope Timmy will be happy and that she will forgive me for what I said. I was sorry that she had to leave so abruptly."

But when she heard the dial tone break in she knew that Timmy's boyfriend had already hung up.

TURN ON GUATEMALA

"Stop that Mark and Peter. Stop all that fighting right now. If you've got nothing better to do with yourselves, try watching the war."

The war our mother had in mind that winter was just a minor thing in Guatemala between some of Ortega's ragged guerrillas and our Rangers. Because it really wasn't major, as those things went, there was always the threat of cancellation, but I guess mom knew that just so long as the feature fighting went on it would always divert us from any mischief—that is, if she let us watch it on the television in the den downstairs. If, for example, she was going out to meet Mr. Dennis, our future stepfather, for the evening, and Markey—who was my senior by two years—was wrestling with me across her bed so that she didn't have any privacy to dress, mom might say: "I wonder what's on TV. Isn't there a war somewhere?" Mom knew those things interested us more than just about anything else. As Mr. Dennis always used to say: "Your mom sure is keen on giving you boys a good time."

One reason why we enjoyed watching war so much is because we both believed that's where daddy must be, even though mom still told us he was in Canada. I mean, we just didn't believe dad would ever do a thing like that. So, whenever mom felt composed enough to leave the house, brother and I would scoot downstairs to the kitchen. Markey would make a plateful of thick BLT's on toast and spread them all gloppy inside with mayo while I mixed us rich, dark pitch-ers full of chocolate or strawberry milk in the blender. Carrying our suppers into the den, we would squat Indian-style before TV for hours, hoping maybe to catch a glimpse of somebody who looked like our dad. But, even if it never happened, that was still okay with us. Just so long as we had a war to watch we were never lonely or gruesome.

As I say, even if it wasn't much of a war in those days, it had its moments. There were lots of those pretty colored flares, and the noises were always sharp, clear, loud, frightening. Since the trouble in Asia they'd fixed up the sound system, and we new kids were lucky to have Captain Jack Smith, a veteran, as announcer, because he grooved with what was happening and could tell about it in a way so that you had to stay glued to the spot. "Well *how* about *that*," the Captain would say. Or, "Hold onto your seats, boys and girls," whenever the action got too much for us. Sometimes he would also shout things: "That was a *great big* Memphis *lollapalooza*," or *"Boy O Boy O Boy."*

Then there were the theme songs, too, of the different sides, all those regiments, battalions, brigades, the marching songs of the counterinsurgents, the irregulars, and their auxiliaries. As I say, there wasn't always a great deal of action going on for a feature, but it was usually very colorful and gripping sort of.

I recall that I enjoyed the way the jet attackers flew no more than fifty yards above the grasslands with their cannon blazing; it made you think they would blast huge holes in the telly with a poof. The magic dragon, that was really something. I always went pale and shrieked whenever they

did it. But Mark's face would turn bright red and he would
sweat and pant and shrink away. He used to cry, "Bam Bam
Bam Hot Damn," and then my big blond brother used to let
me hide my head in his lap until the stretcher-bearers left.
When I looked up again it was always just in time to see
those planes of ours swooshing up to the sky once more with
bushes of oily black smoke rising from where the napalm
fell.

Markey really knew a lot more about wars than I did
and he always said he liked the rockets and the jungle patrols best, all those queer noises, I guess, and, of course, he
dug the big amphib operations. When his best friend Jimmy
MacNamara came to visit, we used to hurry with supper so
we could be in time to catch the pacifications. All those
grubby little people running around frightened for their
lives while our Rangers moved from hut to hut with their
torches—it was really a sight, a sketch, funny, if you know
what I mean, like one of those old-time war movies—and
Mac's dad worked for the TV and he said that wasn't anything compared to what it was like before they invented the
creep camera.

As I say, for city kids like us—with nothing to do and
no place to go now that the streets weren't so safe—war-
watching could be a big deal. I'll never forget those night
patrols when you never knew from one minute to the next
which Ranger's number was up. The glory of it was having
TV work overtime to bring the war to us kids at home. Day
and night that big satellite orbited, glowing with the latest
relays from the front. Except for the commercial breaks, we

had one continual war to watch. Some people said they were doing it for us kids, like a public service. Frankly, I doubt that. A lot of grown-ups liked the programs every bit as much as us. You just couldn't match them.

I think it must have been about the time of my seventh birthday that the trouble also broke out once again in the Middle East. There was fighting galore in the Sinai, the Wilderness of Zin, and the Kuwait Oasis. I'd known ever since age six that I was adopted, which is why I didn't look at all like Markey, so I really rooted big for Jews, but big brother said the damn Arabs were really the underdogs this time and he might just try rooting for them.

We had a couple of big fights about the whole business before we got bored with arguing and agreed to switch back and forth from the guerrilla troubles on ABC to the desert stuff on NBC and CBS. What a gas! Sometimes we would also watch the documentaries on the educational station. Every day they would choose the best from both wars and broadcast the stuff without any commercials at all, after school was over.

That was really something, if you liked their way of doing it. For myself, that's when the serious trouble broke out between Markey and me. He was in junior high already and a bit of a grind, and he said you learned much more about both wars from ETV, but I just liked the way they did it on commercial better because Captain Jack, he was a real surviving veteran and very colorful, and the stuff he gave you was always, or pretty nearly always, in color and almost always live; so you just knew there was no chance for the schoolmarms going snippety-snip with their scissors.

Mom and Mr. Dennis got married the day before Markey's eleventh birthday. I remember that because they were going away to a hotel for a couple of days so they had Cousin June, a college girl, come to stay with us and make us a birthday party with a real homemade chocolate cake from French's with real icing that said:

HAPPY BIRTHDAY MARKEY
MOM, BROTHER & MR. DENNIS

Mom also said that because it was Mark's birthday we could stay up extra late after he blew out the candles. There wasn't any school next day, anyway, because it was the President's birthday. So, after cake and milk, June said she was going upstairs to wash her hair in beer and take a bath and turn down our beds, and wouldn't we like to watch a war for awhile? She said she was fixing to make us chili for lunch tomorrow, but we could only have it if we didn't give her anymore trouble fighting. We never really liked giving June trouble when she was looking after us, especially if it meant losing out on chili, so brother and I went down to the den in our pajamas.

That night there was this new feature on NBC: Street fighting in Atlanta, Georgia. The police were trying to stop *them* before they got to the reservoir. It really wasn't all that exciting—a lot of fire engines and police cars and just a few of the new light tanks. The niggers were losing; that was for sure. They didn't stand a chance against all those police and National Guards, and those new sticky blob things you squirted at them. It was like suicide. Would you believe suicide? By the time mom rang up from her hotel to find out how we were all doing, Markey and I were both pretty bored. He started over to the telly to switch channels.

"This is putting me to sleep," he sneered. "In another minute, I'll be out on my feet. Let's see what's going on with the Rangers."

I remembered how some kids at recess that day were talking about the temporary truce over there and I told brother so.

"Let's just flip the switch anyway," he said, his hand still on the lighted dial. "Maybe there'll be reruns."

Markey turned the dial to ABC just as a commercial was ending.

"Turn on Guatemala," I said.

"Be patient. This is Guatemala. Quiet!"

The screen was now a big gray blank, meaning they were shooting the stuff out in the field. Then a voice: "We return you now to your regularly scheduled program."

Markey and I were staring at a thick gray clump of coffee bushes. Far back, in the undergrowth, came the sound of footsteps. A parrot cried out and a monkey scooted skeedaddle across the picture. A few seconds later this swarthy guy with greasy long hair sticking down from a big straw hat cut his way into view with his machete. He had an A-6 Chicom slung across his right shoulder. Behind him was this dim-looking fat woman, also with an A-6 and an A-4. There were some others following them but we could just barely make out everybody the way they were going single file.

This guy cut his way into view in that little clearing so that he looked like he was no more than maybe fifty yards away from our cameras, and then he just didn't move any closer into focus. He seemed to be afraid to move any closer. He didn't seem sure which way to go. Once he turned around and said something in Spanish to the fat woman, who was really pretty ugly too, but you couldn't hear any of it too clearly because of the way the microphones were hanging. It all just came out sounding like *Hoolaholahula*.

"I wish I knew Spanish," Mark said then. "I think I'll study it next term. It should be a big help when I know what I want to do."

I was still watching the TV with half an eye and trying to listen to my brother. I said: "Mom thinks every language is a big help nowadays . . . I mean, when you work for the TV . . ."

"Just the same," Mark added, "I'm going to learn me some Spanish first."

He pushed a piece of yellow hair off his brow just as the guerrillas were retreating into their cover again.

Now it was very quiet and spooky. Even Captain Jack wasn't saying anything except we could hear him breathing.

It was spooky, and it was also a minor drag.

I asked: "What's happening?"

"Would you believe?" Mark said. "I think that's Ortega. They've set a trap for him. Look. Don't the big odd-ball guy in the hat look like Big Raoul?"

The leader of the guerrillas was starting out of those bushes again, with his A-6 cradled inside his arms. Despite the fact that he was obviously disguised, he sure did seem to resemble the face of the man whom Mark and I had learned all about in 201, he last year and me this one: Raoul Ortega, *El Bicho,* or, as our 201 teacher, Mrs. Wilson, called him, the Red Slob; but you never could be too sure of that because those people, they all look like each other anyway; they're really all pretty slobby.

Still, I was willing to bet even money that it really was Ortega. What a treat! I'd seen that face above the blackboard every day for a year in Mrs. Wilson's classroom. She used to like to point out the long hair covering over the big ears, the big flat nose, too, and the little greasy goat beard. Mrs. Wilson would say: "To many of our Southern good neighbors, children, this man is considered something of a hero. What do we think of him, class?" Some of the PR kids actually had the nerve to shout back: EL BICHO! But most of us knew better. We shouted: SLOB, RED SLOB, RED GANGSTER!

Maybe he was too, but Ortega was also very exciting in a kind of flashy weirdo spick way. I mean, he was such a big, mean-looking guy. Even with all that hair he looked awfully cagey and strong, alert, a regular tiger. We knew all the ways he had ambushed Federals and even some of our counterinsurgents, including the famous Brown Panthers. He lived off the countryside. He recruited from the starving peasants. Crap. It made you creepy just thinking about him. But now that the Rangers were in Guatemala, we were told it was just a matter of time. Anyway, next to that Jewish general with the patch, we both had to admit that he was one of our favorites, although we didn't exactly root for him because he was *the* enemy. But I guess brother and I also knew that if they ever caught up with Ortega that was sure to mean a cancellation of the whole shooting match, and we really didn't care to have that happening to our best show.

So here he was again in the flesh, just about to step out into almost certain death, as Captain Jack would put it, and we sure as shit found ourselves very confused about what we wanted to happen. We could see from the way those helmet pictures were being taken that they had a clear bead on this guy. Could he possibly wangle his way out of such a trap?

Markey and I both crept closer to the screen. It was getting dark. The jungle thickened. We tried to cut the shadows with our eyes, maybe hoping we could, just by hoping, warn Ortega or alert a rescue party. But I'll say this much for him, he looked very cool. Now he was crouching in those bushes with nine or ten of the guerrillas right up next to him. They were all sweat-soaked. He seemed to be holding some kind of council of war.

"I'd give anything," Markey said, "to know what he's saying. Wouldn't you?"

"Do you think," I asked, "he knows what's happening?"

"Don't kid yourself. He knows. They say he's got eyes

everywhere." Mark scratched at his pinkish scalp vigorously. "Boy, I bet even if he doesn't know he's suspicious. Boy, wouldn't you like to know what's going on in his mind now?"

"Wouldn't you like to know, boys and girls?" Captain Jack seemed to be echoing Mark.

A foot crunched against bark. I said: "You want some more birthday cake while we're waiting? I'll go get it for the both of us." Because I was really feeling uptight and just a little dizzy, and I also thought the break might do my fuzzy eyes some good.

Brother said: "Later! Not now!" He seemed a little angry at me for speaking out of turn.

"You just stay where you are," I told him. "I'll go get it."

"Can it," Mark went.

The man we thought was Ortega removed his straw hat. He passed it around so the others could draw lots, like to decide which one would be the first to make a run for it.

"They may run for it," whispered Captain Jack.

Clickety Clack Clik Clik went the slides on the Ranger's safety catches.

"Any minute now . . . another few seconds," throaty Captain Jack said.

High above us, off-mike, the soft low throb of a helicopter.

Mark spoke: "Do you think they'll show us everything this time?"

"I may not watch if they do," I said. "Is that okay with you?"

He giggled.

"Is that okay? Do I have to watch everything?"

"Don't if you're too afraid."

"Markey," June called out from the kitchen, "don't you tease Peter like that. If he doesn't want to watch everything, he doesn't have to. *What's going on in there anyway?*"

A shadow suddenly fell across the dancing carpet. June was standing in the doorway in mom's barbecue apron. *"What's going on tonight?"* she demanded.

To answer risked missing everything. But we were lucky. Just like that, just then, all hell broke loose.

Zap went the guns. *Tat tat tat zap.*

Captain Jack hollered: *"Groovy!"*

Then he hollered: "Say what's happening what's happening there say you what's . . ."

There was this big explosion. Flames everywhere. The spatter of more gunfire. A lot of people started crying all kinds of confusing things.

We couldn't see Ortega anymore because there was too much smoke, but we could hear that steady *thumpthumpthump* like bullets smacking against the bunkers.

Captain Jack was groaning like a hurt animal. Men ran and stumbled, falling forward, spurts of thick dark stuff twisting out of them like pudding mix.

Somebody blew a whistle.

"What's happening?" brother said. "I can't tell what's happening now, can you?"

I had my hands practically over my eyes, but Markey's voice forced me to pull them away. Then the screen cleared so we could see all the bodies. Were they Rangers or guerrillas?

Would you believe? I couldn't tell.

What with the bullets still zapping it didn't prove anything that I didn't see any of Ortega's men running around. Who blew that whistle? The camera swayed back and forth across the scene, like it was out of control.

The camera swayed and jiggled. Nearby some brush was burning. The camera swayed across the burning brush; you could almost smell it. It made me feel just a little sick.

Suddenly Mark screamed: *"Do you think it's all over?"*

I screamed back: *"How should I know?"*

I was really worried about Captain Jack. All those people in front of us were twitching, and the focus was all wrong. Suddenly our screen was full of ghosts.

Then there was another big flame flash and everything went black.

Somebody started to play music.

"Due to circumstances beyond our control we can no longer continue this broadcast."

The next thing we saw was a commercial for Lickety-Splits followed by a film on aqua-skiing in Samoa.

"Flip to ETV," Mark shouted. He was all scrunched up in the darkness. "They'll know for sure what's going on!"

Really I'd had enough of TV of any kind for one evening. I wanted to go to bed, but I didn't like Mark calling me chickenhearted. Creeping over to the screen, I flipped channels.

A man in a blue suit was standing before a pink map of Central America with a pointer.

"It's Rostok all right," Mark said. "Leave it." Because I was now so fed up I was going to flip channels on him again.

I turned up the sound. Rostok wore teenybopper glasses and had a slight lisp. He said: "War is a tragedy, boys and girls, as we all know, but let's not be too sentimental; it can also be a great big comedy of errors. Today near the small village of Ochas Rias on the Southern Front a detachment of our Rangers lay in ambush for Raoul Ortega. We're hoping to have films of that a little later on in this same program.

"Our men were ready to murder *El Bicho*," Rostok said, "dead or alive. What they didn't realize was that Ortega had deployed his main force of guerrillas surrounding us.

"Well, I suppose you could say it's the little miscalculations that hurt worst," Rostok went on. "Poor intelligence work, for one thing, but I suspect we have to give Ortega some credit too. The result: thirty-two Rangers killed and a large number wounded, including our beloved colleague from commercial TV, Captain Jack Smith. Enemy losses were described as heavy but the numbers are not immediately available . . ."

Mark kicked the leg of a chair. Quickly he ran across

to the television and switched off. "Christ," he said, turning, "what a mess. Imagine getting killed by a bunch of Guate-malans . . . *What a fuck-up!*"

He was all red in the face.

Hearing Mark curse, June said: "Your mother wouldn't like to know you talk that way, Markey!"

Then she wagged her finger at both of us: "I don't want you children getting all stirred up about nothing when it's time for bed."

I said, "Okay, June."

"I think I'd like some of that cake now," Mark said. He smiled: "Come on. Join me?"

Really I wasn't feeling very hungry. I guess I was still pretty shook up by all that noise and the jiggling camera picture, the whole confusing mess, all that smoke too so you could almost feel it in your eyes; and the way those people twitched. It wasn't that I was afraid of anything; I was just feeling all stirred up and dizzy inside, like in school when they gave us those light shows.

Really I just wanted to close my eyes to this whole business and snuggle up in the dark opposite Markey in our cozy little beds.

Tomorrow after lunch mom would be back. Maybe she would take us to the park or something. It would be a nice break.

But when I got upstairs, I couldn't get myself to sleep. Markey was all worked up and he still wanted to talk. Ev-erytime I shut him up my eyes closed on that same swaying camera picture. It made me feel a little nauseous. So I let Markey talk some more.

"I really hope we lose this war," he was saying. "The way we're fighting we don't deserve to win."

"Even if we won, then what?" I asked. "There won't be anymore Ortega, that's what."

Mark went: "Yes," and I heard him swallow hard.

There was no other sound.

Then he turned over onto his belly, thrashing at the covers.

Mark asked: "Can you masturbate yet?"

"I'm not ready," I said. "I'm not old enough."

"Yes," he went again, swallowing even harder. "Well I don't like doing it all alone."

He was sitting up now in bed. I could see his face and he looked real angry: "They really oughta get that Ortega. They really oughta go get him," Mark snapped. "I don't like all this silly stuff."

"What silly stuff?"

I was also leaning back in the half-darkness against my elbows. *"What silly stuff, Markey?"*

"The way they fool around and fool around," he said. "They really are hopeless. It's Asia all over again, I tell you. How long have we been watching this war? Crap. It's enough to make you root for Ortega."

Cousin June must have turned out the hall light then because it was very dark all of a sudden in our room and Mark no longer let me sleep with the nightlight. In the inky blackness I must have felt very brave. Otherwise I never would have answered Markey.

Falling back against my bed in the darkness, I spoke words of warning to him.

"Markey, you wouldn't dare to root for Ortega because you know what they say about him in school, Markey, and Mr. Dennis also says that if he wins they'll do terrible things to all of us, even children like you and me . . ."

"What does Mr. Dennis know? He's just mommy's friend."

"He's her husband now," I said, "and he's also our stepfather, and he works for the television . . ."

"Big deal. Everybody works for the television. What makes him so smart about Ortega? I mean, if Ortega really did come here to get us we could always say we'd like to join him. There wouldn't be any law against it then, and that would make a difference, wouldn't it? Because at least they win big once in a while . . ."

"But Markey," I said, "a man like that . . . look what he did to Captain Jack . . . He could do it to you and me. Remember what happened to daddy?"

"He isn't your daddy. *You're adopted*," Mark said. But it didn't hurt that much because I could tell how he was so very upset about losing.

After a minute Mark sat up again: "Look, I'm sorry kid, I didn't mean to punch you out. Can you help it you were adopted? I just meant daddy probably was like all the others, a big weirdo dope. Maybe mom's right, you know. Maybe he did go off to Canada with all the queers."

"Anyway," Mark said, "you heard Rostok. He said the whole thing is like a comedy of errors. Well, I say maybe so, but I also say that if you're not man enough to take on Ortega you better give up. I say I'm sick of watching us get licked by Guatemala and the rest of those nitwit nations and if daddy were here tonight I'd tell him so too. But you know what I think? I think daddy *was* a queer. Like mom and Mr. Dennis say . . ."

"Don't say that . . ."

"Who's bossing me around?" Mark asked. HOW CAN YOU STAND BEING BEATEN ALL THE TIME?

"But we kill a lot of them too."

"Isn't that something. We kill them and they kill us and I'm supposed to think that's a big deal. Well, I say fuck them and fuck them good. Daddy was no hero, I'll tell you that much, or he would have creamed Ortega, who is creaming us . . . HE'S CREAMING US, HE'S HOSING US, DON'T YOU SEE?

"Mark," I went, "stop that. Suppose somebody hears. June might be listening . . ."

SHIT ON JUNE . . .

"Mommy wouldn't like it if people knew you said such things," I began. "You know how it is with her at the office . . ."

Mark interrupted me with bitter laughter: "Mr. Dennis will take care of mommy. Go to sleep, will you?"

I finally did fall asleep and dreamed that Mark was right all along: Ortega *was* winning the war. He was standing in our living room, pointing a rifle at Mark and me. "I killed your daddy," he said to Mark. *"And yours too!"*

Early in the morning the sound of Mark masturbating woke me, but by the time I looked up he was finished and had fled the room.

It was very gray. I was all alone in my bed in a cold gray sweat. The room was plain empty.

Downstairs the television was already making noises. When I leaned over the bannister to look into the den, I saw Mark crouching before the glowing picture.

I knew right away then, that we were looking at the face of a dead man. A neat black hole pitted his forehead. The eyes were staring open, the mouth wide open too, and sort of black inside. A fly buzzed across the flat, broad nose.

It took another few seconds before I was certain this was Ortega.

Inside my stomach I felt a tiny pinprick. Ortega looked very ugly, but not at all frightening. He seemed like he was surprised to be on TV that way in our den. I wondered whether it was okay to feel sorry for him now.

"Come on down," Mark cried out then, hearing my footsteps creak. "It's not as bad as I thought it was. Look who they got. They got him after all. Rostok says he was dressed up like a pregnant woman. They didn't take any chances with him this time. They won't even show you his body because it got all burned from the neck down, but *that's him all right. Look!"*

I came up even closer to the screen. Sure it was him all right. He didn't even look mean or weird, but I just couldn't feel too sorry for him.

After a little while my lids were all numb.

I asked: "Does that mean the war is over?"

"Not so fast," Mark said. "Not so fast."

He was smiling. He was smiling nice at me again. He seemed very calm and I felt sort of calm too. Nice.

When mom came home she and Mr. Dennis took Mark to the zoo, but I stayed home in bed.

LAW 'N ORDER DAY

Cousin June and Cousin Minny was having nervous breakdowns. You could see it all over their faces. Also from the way they talked to each other.

"My fear is," Cousin Minny said, "everybody is out there protesting one thing or another. An' I'm not protesting anything."

"You wait girl," said Cousin June, "you will."

"What I got to protest for?" asked Minny. "Ain't got a blessed thing . . ."

"What about them Gotleibs?"

Minny looked cross: "You leave them outta this, hear?"

June sneered.

A mouth full of pink and white was June's sneer. Like Minny, she wore her hair natural, didn't use any more of those messy creams. Cousin June was our block captain for Justice. She just had to be blacker and cleaner than anybody else.

She said: "Minny, what you got to be so edgy about? Got no stickers to stick? Why you so edgy like that Minny? You just like one of us. You got your stickers and the Negative Income Tax. With you it should all be bonnyroo."

No use telling that to Minny; she wasn't convinced. For one thing, she was cream yellow, much too light. Also, she was just naturally edgy with Bascomb in the Police out there in Bellflower and Eldridge serving against the Thai

Viet. "Everybody out there protesting," she repeated. "For that reason alone I could end up in the crazy hospital."

"Girl, you sure are crazy if you believe that," went June. She handed Minny two fresh packets of Stars 'n Stripes stickers: "Be sure you use plenty of wet tongue this time, *hear?*"

It was our second Law 'N Order Day in as many months. On our block a holiday spirit prevailed. The men home on leaves from Rehab Heaven lounged about in their fatigue uniforms, sipping beer in the hot sun and chatting to each other in Swahili. There was light smog in the Basin, but all over the streets of Freedom City oleanders, pomanders, magnolias, and flaming eucalyptus was blooming.

Later in the day there would be a Biafran Relief Picnic in Karenga Park. On Medgar Evers Boulevard a new soul food restaurant was fixing to open. Displays of bunting, fireworks, a parade, a light show, a freakout with joints. The whole works! There was even this giant searchlight, just like they have when they open an Orange Julius for white folks. Weakly, it glared at the hot blue sky of Southland.

For the folks in Pacoima, Anaheim, Bellflower, and Pantages it was just another holiday; maybe you fidgeted in the garden, and maybe you played golf. Not for brothers and sisters like us. Sitting around in the kitchen over coffee waiting for Burner to change into his costume, June, Minny, and Yours Truly felt it right in the pits of their stomachs. It was what they call *refu*—deep. Every once in

awhile poor old June would show her edges, look up from
her cup, and holler: "What's keeping you Burner?"

"Just looking for my mojo," he shouted back.

Then: "Baby, you seen my molotovs anywhere?"

"They is on the back porch where the social workers
left them," June declared. "And be sure you wear your as-
bestos."

"I dig."

"Well, alright," June said, "but just you hurry.
Minny's getting edgy and so is the boy. You sure are a
slow-poke."

Cousin June went to the stove and poured herself a
second cup of coffee.

Then Minny said: "I feels terrible about the Gotleibs . . ."

June snorted: "Just what you got to feel so terrible
about them?"

"I mean," Minny went, "they coming home to such a
messy apartment . . ."

"Broom worries! Is that all?" June gasped.

Then Burner appeared, and Minny and I was gasping
right along with her.

Burner was togged in a red rubber scooby, a face mask,
oxygen tubes, high red rubber boots. Six or seven molotovs
on a bandolier was strung across his chest, he carried his
Black Power trident and had a strand of bronze *ushujaa* bells
around his neck which made him tinkle when he walked.

"Sure is hot," Burner said, going to the icebox for a beer with a tinkle-tinkle.

June said: "Drink up quick. You only got but a minute."

She looked him up and down to make sure he was the way he should be, and smiled real easy at him, for a sec, less-edgy-seeming, and tense.

"Every time you do it, suits you better." She smiled. "You sure beginning to fit the part, Burner."

He raised his mask to smile back. "Guess I like's to make it hot for some folks," he chuckled. Chuckling softly to himself, Burner added: "Blauveldt been around yet?"

"Not yet," said Minny.

"He will be," June added.

"Sure," said Burner, "he wouldn't miss a trick like this for anything."

Blauveldt was a professor from the Human Relations Division of the L.A.P.D. If you want to know who dreamed up the whole idea of Law 'N Order Day in the first place, it just had to be Blauveldt. Skinny, scrawny, white, punky, with long hair and bad teeth, Blauveldt taught Caucasian Studies nights at the Free University. During the days he worked as a Consultant to the Pigs, dreaming up ways to "legitimize" our anger. Some said it didn't end there. According to them, Blauveldt was really the works. Would you believe that? Anyway, nobody much liked or trusted him, but they all agreed he had plenty of smarts. Blauveldt hated white folks worse than any of us, and that was some big whole lot too. It was Blauveldt who took Burner off the

Welfare. He give him this "employment of last resort."
Officiating over Law 'N Order days was the Social Workers' idea, but Blauveldt ran the Social Workers which ran
the Police. That little Jewy brain knew every angle, let me
tell you.

The usual number on Law 'N Order Day was for the
Justice Committee to choose an oppressor. Then Blauveldt
would drop down by helicopter right alongside of our orna-
mental orange tree. While Cousin June and Minny was
licking their stickers on all the car windows, Blauveldt and
Burner—along with a gang of Social Workers and nonpro-
fessionals—would go direct to the oppressor's store so as to
light their fires. If the blaze grew bright enough, everybody
in Freedom City would come running from their houses
and stoops so the L.A.P.D. boys could go right in through
the front doors to search for hidden weapons. About an hour
later Chungwa would sound the all-clear signal. With the
Jew store reduced to ashes, Burner would poke about with
his trident for mojos, black cat bones, and what-nots. Then
the crowd would break apart. There would be a block
party. Mayor Rafferty would speak. Once even the President . . .

That's how it had been for ten years now, ever since
the time of the Big Massacres, and that's how we all liked it
to be, but the fact was we was fast running out of Jew
stores. Besides, Minny was right: The protests weren't
helping any to keep folks calm.

The reason for the protests was, as usual, the Power Structure. Some people said Blauveldt and Burner was now agents of the Power Structure and they just had to go too. There was a passel of grumbling. It wasn't all just sour grapes. Some people said they just wanted to burn anything they pleased, like in the old days. Not just oppressors. Why not Chicanos or Japs? Who is to say what's what when it comes to burning? Also, there was getting to be a regular Jew-scarcity in Freedom City.

That's why we were so relieved when Burner spoke up: "I think we going to catch ourselves a couple of white-eye schoolteachers this time."

I asked: "You think the Mayor will let you?"

"Just so long as they's Jews," went Cousin June, with a smile.

A sound truck was starting down our block toward Pomander:

> *Border to border*
> *Law and order.*
> *If you yearning*
> *For a little burning*
> *Have yourself a ball*
> *With Law 'N Order . . . an all . . .*

As the truck turned onto Selma the music faded. The next sec we heard the dull throbs of a roto blade. A big red whirlybird cropped into view on our front lawn. Blauveldt was here.

"Well well well," he smiled, broadly, pulling up the sleeves of his orange jump suit as he stood in our front door: "Another day . . . another dollar . . . and dig this: *Word from City Hall is it's groovy with the teachers and firemen only leave the Pigs alone, you dig?* The Pigs have got to be A-*all*-alone. Hardly any white pigs left on the force anyways so I don't think that should hurt us too much. The same goes for fireboys. Ever hear of a Jew fireman? Well, I never did and I'm one of them. Which is why," he added, lighting himself a joint, "I think we'll do us a schoolteacher."

"School's closed today," I said. "It's a holiday . . ."

"The boy's right," said June.

"*So?*" Burner added. "*How we going to get one of them if school is closed . . . ?*"

"He got a point there," went Minny. "All this protesting one thing or another . . . and this boy, he got a point there . . ."

One thing about Blauveldt: Nothing which he isn't hip to. Pulling softly on his joint, the eyes go soft and squinty. "*Who controls the school board?*" he asked. "*You do! So there's no reason why you can't telephone a couple of those honkies and say: 'Get your ass down here to a meeting.'*"

"Sure enough," went Burner, after a little while. He really admired Blauveldt, even though he was a Cau-Cau.

Then Cousin June said: "I'll call Mr. Rubin . . . and Dr. Hoffman . . ."

"Groovy," Blauveldt said. "And why not get that girl who teaches Shakespeare at Martin Luther King? The one with the nice soft buns. I hear she balls her students . . ."

"Just like one of them!" Minny went.

"Sure enough," went Burner a second time.

It was all arranged: One by one Cousin June dialed each of the teachers and told them how she expected to meet them in half an hour at the Vest Pocket Renewal Park on the corner of Lupine and Emmit Till. Then Burner and Blauveldt went off to raise a mob, and June and Minny, with me, did some more sticker-pasting up and down the blocks.

"All this protesting," Minny kept saying, "don't seem like it leads nowhere except to that crazy house," but she bowed her old gray head and licked and stuck and licked and stuck again until the Stars 'n Stripes was on every single car windshield for four or more blocks around.

It was two in the afternoon before we caught the first smells of burning white flesh. Ten minutes later greasy black flame was licking the sky above Lupine and Till. On a bullhorn we could hear the voice of Burner.

I'LL TORCH YOUR WHITE ASSES . . . TORCH YOUR HONKY WHITE JEW ASSES . . .

SOCK IT TO EM BLOOD, went the crowd. SOCK IT TO EM BURNER BROTHER.

There followed three dull shrieks, a raucous bellow, then silence. Flames were crackling high up above the

Watts Towers. In another minute THE MOTHERWITS
commenced to make music.

That evening we sat around until midnight waiting for
Blauveldt with his police reports. Outside, dancing under
the trees was unflagging. Clots of music burst against my
ears. While Cousin June and Cousin Minny knitted,
Burner dabbed petroleum jelly on his scorches.

Somewhere around ten o'clock Bascomb called from
Bellflower. Folks there had seen it all on television. They
was impressed.

That made Minny feel a whole lot better. She thought
of calling the Gotleibs to ask if she could give them the half-
day tomorrow and Friday, but decided against it: "Seeing it
was Law 'N Order Day, they probably stayed out in Palm
Springs."

I was feeling nice and groggy and sleepy because it
was such a long day and I had school tomorrow. I could tell
the grown-ups thought I should be in bed, but I wanted to
hear what the Pigs had to say.

At quarter to midnight Cousin June yawned and got
up to make a fresh pot of coffee. Then she turned on TV.
Mr. President was speaking to the nation. As far as we
knew he'd been speaking all evening long again. Looked
very old and tired, not much like his usual self. All along his
chin were those heavy shadows.

"My administration," he was saying, "never will be
hostile to the legitimate aspirations of the black man. We

seek to encourage black capitalism, to channel black anger into legitimate paths. Law 'N Order days like this just go to prove that Law 'N Order can mean Law 'N Order, with profits. Let's not sow the seeds of discord unless we wish to reap a crop of fires, but if the burning blossoms forth again remember there's a little bit of hell in all of us Americans and we're all Americans together.

"My administration stands for Justice," Mr. President added. "We will never be hostile to the legitimate aspirations of black people, but we wish to remind all of you *out there in Freedom City, U.S.A.*, that if you cry fire in a crowded theater you won't be able to watch the movie."

"Yes, my administration is as Black Power as the next guy's," said the man they call Mr. President. "Baby, light my fire because *you got to fight fire with fire.*"

Sometimes I think there isn't any real Mr. President. They just have this recording of him and his Mrs. That's what I happen to think. I mean, you watch the television and there are all those long-haired generals and admirals and senators, and there he is—this Mr. President—telling it like it is, all day long. Making speeches! Who is running things meanwhile? Must be Blauveldt.

"Just like a Jew, ain't it," Cousin June says. She says that once the white men owned Wall Street and Wall Street owned the world, but after what happen in Asia they decided to get out of business and they give it all to a Jew name Fard. Now all they do is sit around and smoke pot and screw like colored folks and act scared, all except the Jews who just like to work and oppress all the time (which is why they have to go), and their leaders are Blauveldt and the Police who are the Social Workers, only nobody knows for sure if this is really true because the President is always on television and he won't answer any questions. What with the capital now in San Marino, it's hard to figure just what any man thinks he's doing.

Confusing? You bet your ass it is. Black people are more confused by white jive than ever. Only some people tell us we have power, and I guess we do, what with another War Against Poverty too, and you just know you wouldn't have any such thing if it hadn't been for what white folks thought about black people.

Besides, Blauveldt says we do have power. He is always coming here first when he has a Police report to make. Tonight Blauveldt said: "The Pigs say you are all clean. Spread it around among the brothers . . ."

Cousin June was so happy she was grinning from every crease in her face: "I guess this just has to be the best Law 'N Order Day ever . . ."

"Just you wait until next month," Blauveldt declared.

Burner looked up wide-eyed: "What you going to do then?"

"Not me . . . *you*." Blauveldt smiled. *"Next month you going to burn me . . . and the President . . ."*

"Fat chance," went Cousin June.

"No, baby, he means it." Burner was grinning. Only he had gotten Blauveldt's point. "Do you really mean it?

You not shitting?" he asked. *"You really going to let us do our thing?"*

"How can I help it?" Blauveldt shrugged.

Then Cousin June said: "You got a lot of smarts Blauveldt. Sometimes I think you the only white man left who knows where it's really at . . ."

"Thank you."

Blauveldt was about to light himself a fresh joint when Minny suddenly spoke out: "Everybody do seem to be protesting one thing or another, and I just don't happen to be protesting anything."

"Why don't you go lick a flag?" Blauveldt said.

Which made Burner declare: WATCH THE WAY YOU TALK TO BLACK WOMANHOOD, JEW-BOY!

The phone rang.

It was the President.

He was making Bascomb Chief of Police.

"Just in the nick of time," said Blauveldt.

Said Burner: "Think I'd like to be Secretary of State someday."

Said Blauveldt: "You just keep on legitimizing your anger and I know I could get you that HEW job."

Said Cousin June: "Burner wouldn't like all those poor folks pestering him all the time."

Said Blauveldt: "Can't say I blame him."

He opened a pocket in his jump suit and found a tin of cyanide pills. "The only thing that ever puts me to sleep." He grinned.

"So," he continued, "Bascomb is going to be The Chief of Police, which is the same as being head Social Worker. Ever wonder what that makes me?"

"Sure enough," Cousin June popped in. *"That means your days are numbered, white eyes."*

"Quite! I quite agree!" Blauveldt took two dexes, an amy, and a cyanide pill, and said, "Wop Bop A Loo Bop!"

Once again everything was bonnyroo in Freedom City.

Afterword

I write my little stories in between the novels, like a man twitching his toes with his eyes open, though he thinks he is asleep.

After each long work there is usually a dull period during which I enjoy nothing so much as eating sawdust. Sometimes a story or two will interrupt, like the hiccoughs.

While I am writing a story it is usually my whole life to me (and I take that very seriously), but often, afterward, I have the feeling that I have been locked inside the lavatory of a certain hijacked airliner by Cuban counterrevolutionaries who are bound from Kennedy Airport for Newark.

The forms I choose permit a commendable brevity and terseness which has the same advantage for me that it does for the reader: it is simply not necessary to dawdle over these, much less swelter. Wherever possible, I have tried not to include any of the bad trips I've taken, though they may be equally as brief. I guess I still believe in the redemptive qualities of fiction, the way any good stand-up comic believes in his jokes.

Writing a novel for me has always been going three steps backward and two steps forward. In the stories I find I rarely have the time, or need, to reverse gears. Unless I am prepared to go from beginning to end, all in the course of a single day, I rarely complete the draft.

If some of these stories are very very short that means it was rather a long day with lots of spaces in between for eating sawdust.

The earliest of the earlies is "Timmy," and I include it here because I regard some things about the mood of the piece as the mother of us all. When I started twitching a lot recently, I threw out many of the longer things I'd written and published earlier in magazines because they seemed to have been done by a very snotty young man with whom I had only recently quarreled.

I would like to say it is very nice of Charles Scribner's Sons to let me publish a collection of sawdust hiccoughs. If you know any man or woman with similar problems, may I recommend a class in creative writing such as is being offered at most colleges, universities, and junior colleges.

MARCH 30, 1972

About the Author

Richard Elman has published five novels, the most recent FREDI & SHIRL & THE KIDS. Besides AN EDUCATION IN BLOOD, his novels include the trilogy: THE 28TH DAY OF ELUL, LILO'S DIARY, and THE RECKONING. He is also the author of two non-fiction books, THE POORHOUSE STATE and ILL-AT-EASE IN COMPTON, and co-editor of CHARLES BOOTH'S LONDON.